STRENGTH ENDURING

A Talon Pack Novel

CARRIE ANN RYAN

STRENGTH ENDURING

A Thick Pick Novel

CARRIE ANN RYAN

Strength Enduring
A Talon Pack Novel
By: Carrie Ann Ryan
© 2018 Carrie Ann Ryan
ISBN: 978-1-943123-88-9

Cover Art by Charity Hendry

For more information, please join Carrie Ann Ryan's MAILING LIST.
To interact with Carrie Ann Ryan, you can join her FAN CLUB.

PRAISE FOR CARRIE ANN RYAN

"Carrie Ann Ryan knows how to pull your heartstrings and make your pulse pound! Her wonderful Redwood Pack series will draw you in and keep you reading long into the night. I can't wait to see what comes next with the new generation, the Talons. Keep them coming, Carrie Ann!" – Lara Adrian, New York Times bestselling author of CRAVE THE NIGHT

"Carrie Ann Ryan never fails to draw readers in with passion, raw sensuality, and characters that pop off the page. Any book by Carrie Ann is an absolute treat." – New York Times Bestselling Author J. Kenner

"With snarky humor, sizzling love scenes, and brilliant, imaginative worldbuilding, The Dante's Circle series reads as if Carrie Ann Ryan peeked at my personal wish list!" – NYT Bestselling Author, Larissa Ione

"Carrie Ann Ryan writes sexy shifters in a world full of passionate happily-ever-afters." – *New York Times* Bestselling Author Vivian Arend

"Carrie Ann's books are sexy with characters you can't help but love from page one. They are heat and heart blended to perfection." *New York Times* Bestselling Author Jayne Rylon

Carrie Ann Ryan's books are wickedly funny and deliciously hot, with plenty of twists to keep you guessing.

They'll keep you up all night!" USA Today Bestselling Author Cari Quinn

"Once again, Carrie Ann Ryan knocks the Dante's Circle series out of the park. The queen of hot, sexy, enthralling paranormal romance, Carrie Ann is an author not to miss!" *New York Times* bestselling Author Marie Harte

DEDICATION

To my readers.
Thank you for still loving my wolves.

ACKNOWLEDGMENTS

With every book comes a time where I feel like I need to scream at my characters and yet I know that I'll find my way out of the abyss.

Writing a book might be a solitary adventure, but I know that in some respects I am never alone.

Chelle - Thank you for being my sounding board and my wonderful editor.

Charity- Thank you for the amazing cover.

Stacey and Kennedy - Thank you for coffee every morning so I can find the energy and the worlds to write all the words.

Viv - Thank you for sitting down with me and plotting. I totally needed it.

To the group of women I talk to daily about business and mental health - Thank you for knowing when I needed you and when I needed to breathe.

To my readers - Thank you again for being with me in this world for years and never backing away. The Talons aren't finished yet and I know that's because of you.

To Dan - I love you and miss you every day. I wish you were here to read this one like all the rest.

Happy Reading,

Carrie Ann

STRENGTH ENDURING

In the penultimate novel of the Talon Pack series from NYT Bestselling Author Carrie Ann Ryan, an Enforcer must make the ultimate choice when it comes to a human woman with a secret she doesn't know she holds.

Kameron Brentwood has only one thing on his mind: defeating the enemy. He doesn't have time for a human woman who sets his teeth on edge and makes his wolf prowl. It shouldn't matter that she's his mate because he's always thought that mating is a distraction. Yet as soon as he gets to know the woman, he figures out that there's no hiding from the attraction he feels for her.

Dhanielle Coburn has always been on the outside looking in when it comes to the Talon Pack, but she's not about to let fate and the moon goddess decide her path for her. If and when she takes Kameron as a mate, it will be *her* choice. Yet when she suddenly finds herself in the

Pack's inner sanctum, deeper than she ever thought possible, she has to fight not only her need for the man in front of her but also a hidden secret about her family she didn't even know she had.

When the choice is pulled from both of their hands, the two will need to learn who they are apart, and who they can be together. Because there's more to mating than a mark and a prophecy that has come back to haunt them. And even though they may be fated, the ultimate sacrifice just might take them both in the end.

CHOICE

Dreams had been a part of her life since before she could speak. She'd seen countless first breaths, myriad final ones. She'd seen war, triumph, agony, and despair. And through it all, she'd known that few things could change the outcomes of the dreams she had.

And only true patience and sacrifice could change the dreams she bore when she woke.

The birth had gone well, her daughter screaming through the pain but using her strength of will and character to bring forth new life into the world. Her son-in-law had been the one to hold his wife, coaching her through the panic and stress, but had taken as much pain as he was able.

His powers could only do so much in the face of what was natural, what was good.

And when the one who dreamed, the one who had

watched her daughter bring life, was there to guide the new baby from its mother's womb, she hadn't had time to weep, no chance to breathe.

In an instant, she dreamed, but didn't dream. She saw years pass, saw the beauty in the moment, the strength of the girl who would one day be a woman in her arms. She saw the power of the magic within her veins, the worth of her soul and heart.

Then she saw the sacrifice that would be made.

The terror that would ebb.

And the loss that would come when they failed.

The witch who now held her granddaughter didn't speak for a full minute as she cradled the new life, though in her waking dreams, decades passed. Her daughter and her son-in-law didn't say a word, their eyes focused on the witch and their new child. They had seen the woman in her dreamstate before, knew that waking her would mean changing fate in ways that were far more than unpredictable.

But then the witch opened her eyes and looked down at the purity in her hands, the hope that could be if one demanded it, and knew what she had to do. She looked up at her daughter and the son of her heart and smiled.

Then she lied.

Later, when the new parents held their baby, the now-grandmother gathered her supplies, knowing what must be done. It would hurt, it would shatter the trust before them, but she knew the path that would come. There was still hope in the darkness, still a light she could beg for.

And because of that hope, she would hold her grand-daughter one last time.

As her daughter and son-in-law slept, the witch who dreamed stood above them, wrapping the two in an embrace of love and magic. They let out shocked gasps in their slumber, but she knew what must come next, for they wouldn't remember the whys of it in the morning. They wouldn't remember much of anything having to do with a certain part of their lives at all.

That was one good reason their kind was so far away from the others of their powers. If there were more, the grandmother might not have been able to do what came next.

Then she went to her granddaughter's room and held her close, rocking the babe in her arms as tears slid silently down her cheeks.

"Stand up," she whispered.

"Open up." She kissed the baby's cheek.

"Give up." She set the child down.

"Sacrifice begets sacrifice."

And as the baby stared at her with eyes far older than she should have at her age, the grandmother opened her arms, letting the magic run through her, doing what must be done.

And then she was no more. Not even a memory.

But the child slept under the moonlight, as did her parents in the next room. And when they woke, they couldn't mourn what they did not know, couldn't reach inside and touch a power that had once held them close.

For it was no more.

But along the wind, a whisper would come, and a child would grow, and a grandmother with tears in her eyes would be remembered...if only the magic so chose.

CHAPTER ONE

Kameron Brentwood's fist smashed into the rogue's face, the bones in the wolf's cheek cracking beneath his clenched fingers as he gritted his teeth, his own bones aching at the contact. This wolf, this man, had once been part of another Pack on the other side of the world, had once been a functioning member of society. Then the world, the Pack's bonds, and the rogue's own wolf had all become too tangled in a web of strain and panic, and the man had lost control of the wolf entirely.

It was Kameron's job to take care of the rogues near the Talon Pack wards. At least the ones that didn't come to the Pack looking to take out the Alpha. Those, Gideon—his brother and Alpha—had to deal with himself. The leader couldn't ignore a challenge according to Pack law.

Because this particular wolf had gone too far and had

not only killed his family but also a human along the way, there was no hope for redemption. No way for a life to continue under the continued watch of the world and their own needs as wolves.

The rogue in human form stumbled to the ground, his eyes all wolf, no longer able to shift fully because he'd broken far beyond redemption.

And with one quick movement, Kameron reached out and snapped the rogue's neck, the sound echoing through the trees.

Now, Kameron was alone in the forest, only the sound of his own heartbeat filling his ears as the animals around them had gone silent in the presence of two predators. He slowly let the man who had once been an honored and strong member of his Pack fall to the ground, with Kam's hand under the other man's head so he wouldn't land too hard. There may not be pain anymore, but that didn't mean Kameron would let the man end without dignity. The other Alpha had let Kameron and his people know that this rogue might be on the way as they'd been trying to track his movements for over a year now. Somehow, even without control, the broken wolf had been able to evade them all. Except Kameron.

Because Kameron was the Enforcer of the Talon Pack. One of the strongest wolves in the area, and one of the best Enforcers in the world.

And he'd just killed a man because of his duty.

He let out a breath, running a hand over his face before growling. He looked down at his bruised knuckles. Little blood covered his hands visibly, but he could still see the invisible, red trails on the tan of his skin.

He'd barely broken a sweat taking out the rogue, and as he called his people to help clean up the mess, he knew he'd have to run out the rest of his energy or he'd end up hurting someone in practice later on. That was the problem when his emotions ran high like this. The Pack and his family thought him the man of ice, the man of such control that he felt nothing. He never let others see his emotions, never let them feel them through the Pack bonds, but they were there.

And he hated every damn one.

Once his crew came in to take the body so they could send him back to his Pack for a proper burial, Kameron went around the perimeter again to ensure that the den was still safe. The war with the humans was over, and thanks to new treaties and laws, their land was safe from satellites and prying eyes—at least for the time being—but that wasn't the only thing he was checking for. The Aspens had been quiet for too long, and Kameron hadn't been able to get ahold of their contact, Audrey, who was also the Aspen Pack's Beta.

He'd known as soon as she helped his brother and sister-in-law, betraying the secrets of her Pack in the process, that things wouldn't end well, but he still felt responsible for what happened to her.

Even as he thought that, it wasn't Audrey that drifted through his mind. No, it was another woman, a human with a sweet and delectable scent that refused to leave his thoughts. He didn't want to think about Dhani and what

7

that scent meant, so he wouldn't. The more he did, the less focused he would be. And with yet another war on the horizon, he had to be sure he was strong enough to lead his team and follow his brother, his Alpha, onto the battlefield.

A human with a sharp tongue and a delectable scent would only complicate matters.

His wolf pawed at him, annoyed that he was ignoring what was right in his face, but it wasn't as if he could stop what he was doing and follow the promise of a connection that could turn out to be nothing. He'd seen the way losing focus could hurt a Pack, and the Talons relied on him for their protection. He couldn't let his attention wander to something sweeter—not with the Aspens and their insane Alpha, Blade, hiding so close somewhere in their woods.

He couldn't scent them, and knew they weren't there at the moment, but they'd be back. Watching. They always were. And when they came back again, Kameron would take them out. He wouldn't allow anyone to hurt what was his. Not again.

And even if it took all he was, even if he had to push away anything that could have been another connection, he'd do it. Because saving his Pack and keeping Blade and his ilk away was all that mattered.

He let out a growl when his wolf huffed at him, annoyed by his train of thoughts. His wolf would just have to get over whatever it was currently feeling. Kameron had, after all. Or at least he was trying.

He knew he wasn't being fair and was most likely being so pigheaded that he was going to get himself in trouble, but it wasn't as if he could change the way he'd thought his whole life. Especially not because of one scent that wouldn't leave his mind.

It would be safer for everyone if he focused on the threat at hand and then saw if fate were truly testing him when it came to a certain woman. That wasn't how it worked for most wolves, but Kameron wasn't most wolves. He knew his other half and could control it better than most of the Pack could with theirs, and that meant they'd come to an understanding. And when the time came, and if Dhani truly were his mate, he'd try to figure out the next step. Dhani was smart and would understand why he had to stay away in order to keep his focus on the enemy and not be distracted by something that could change the way he thought and fought.

And, once again, he knew he wasn't as convincing as he needed to be. But he couldn't change his plans now.

"I'm an idiot," he growled, then went back to his patrol. He needed to go back inside the den wards soon to have dinner with his family, and that meant he only had an hour or so left of being on high-alert and trying to get that scent and what it meant out of his mind. At the moment, he was still on Pack land, meaning there shouldn't be anyone who wasn't Talon or a guest of the Talons anywhere near. The fact that there had been a rogue wolf earlier just set his own wolf on edge. He knew the night wasn't over. The warded area of the den was what hid their people from view. The wards themselves didn't stretch out across the entire Pack land, as that would be far too vast and taxing on the witches and magic that held the wards in place. So that meant there were layers of patrols on each section of the perimeter, ensuring that they were doing their best to keep their land safe.

He stalked around for a few more minutes until an unfamiliar and very *human* scent drifted to him. He held back a growl. He knew of only three humans—one of them not so human anymore—who were allowed on Pack land, and this scent didn't belong to any of them.

Kameron didn't let his claws slide through his fingertips like his wolf wanted him to do since this human could just be a lost hiker or some other crap like that. The last thing his Pack needed right then was the bad publicity of having a scared, lost human come up on a wolf in human form yet with claws out that could draw blood.

His people had to constantly toe the lie of standing up for themselves and showing their strength, and not scaring the humans that thought the shifters were monsters.

Kameron really didn't care either way, but then again, that's why he wasn't part of the Pack's public persona.

He was the one who hid in the shadows for their protection. They didn't want him out in the real world, scaring unsuspecting tourists with his sharp fangs.

So he kept his fangs and claws in check but carefully followed the scent, coming up on the human in a short jean skirt, boots, and a top that didn't cover enough skin to do any good. Considering that the weather up in the mountains and forest wasn't the warmest, he had no idea what this woman was doing here.

"Lost?" he asked, his voice a growl. He didn't try to change it, though. She was on Pack territory, and while he wouldn't try to scare her too much, there were boundaries marked for a reason. They had pups close by, for the goddess's sake. He wasn't about to let them come to harm from what looked like a too-curious human.

The woman turned on her heel, almost fell, then righted herself in the next instant. When she got a look at him, her eyes widened for a moment, then narrowed into an almost sultry expression.

Well, fuck. He had a feeling he knew why she was here, and he was not in the mood to deal with her. She wasn't the first, and with how his day was going, she wouldn't be the last either.

"Oh, I'm so glad I found you. I was looking for someone just like you."

Kameron didn't let his guard down even though she sounded sweet as pie. They'd had problems with humans from a new faction where—man or woman—they came onto Pack land, trying to seduce answers out of wolves in order to figure out how to take them out. Misguidedly, they thought of shifters as messengers of evil.

"You're trespassing on Talon land. You better have a good reason, or I'm either sending you to the human authorities or somewhere the Pack can deal with you." He didn't tell her that he'd take her to the newly built holding facility they now had where they could interrogate trespassers. It was a good way to keep those not Pack away from the den, and keep the Alpha safe in case Gideon had to come and deal with the humans themselves.

Lost hikers, or in this woman's case, groupies, got sent home right away. Because while he hadn't known her scent, now that he got a good look at her, he knew her face. One of his men had taken a photo of her the last time she came onto Pack land so the others would know to watch out for her.

Some humans wanted shifters dead simply for being what they called abominations. Others wanted to protect them as if they were an endangered species. Still others desired a world where they could live their lives as if they were normal.

And some, like this woman, wanted to fuck a shifter to say they could.

This was why he hated people. Human, shifter, witch, or whatever else was out there. He hated them all. Hence why people thought him a grouchy asshole. He lived up to that reputation well.

"You've been warned before," he added before she could plead her case. "This is the second warning. We don't give thirds."

They had treaties with the human government. Their land was protected, and what happened in their territory in protection of their people was under the shifters' jurisdiction. Yes, the human faction who wanted all shifters tagged or killed would always have a problem with anything done on Pack land, but as of right then, human laws were on the Pack's side.

And that meant the human in front of him was on her last free pass.

He'd already had to kill one person today; he didn't want to make it a second.

She licked her lips, but it did nothing for him. His wolf wanted their human, not this one. Not that he was going to allow his wolf to think of Dhani as *theirs* again.

"I just wanted to…well, I guess you know what I wanted to see. I'm not harming anyone. There's no law saying I can't…flirt with a wolf."

He barely resisted the urge to roll his eyes. "No, there isn't. But there *are* laws about trespassing on our land. You want to bag a wolf? Go to a shifter bar like all the other people who want to find someone to hook up with or be with or whatever your end game is. Coming here isn't helping anyone." Not that there were actually shifter bars. But there were bars in the human world that his people hung out at when they weren't on duty, and when times were safer for them to be away from the den. It had taken too many years and struggles for them to have that freedom, and it was one of Kameron's duties to ensure that they were able to keep it.

He also hated the fact that he was having this conversation at all. He didn't care what this woman did. She was an adult, and the choices she made in life were hers alone. He just hated that she had to come onto Pack land to do it.

"Come on, I'll walk you back to your car."

She sighed but didn't bother trying to flirt with him again. She knew there was no reason to. She wasn't the first groupie—a term the men and women came up with them-selves—and she wouldn't be the last. Kameron just wanted no part in it.

By the time he silently got her to her car, which she'd parked in a makeshift lot on the edge of their territory, he was running late for the end of his shift and just wanted to go home and not think about stupid people making stupid decisions. Hence why he really wasn't in the mood for the other car pulling into the dirt parking lot. And, because of that, he was probably going to be more of an asshole than usual.

"You're going to want to drive back. You're on the edge of Talon land, and there's no going forward from here."

The man with the recorder in his hand shook, but he didn't back away. "I only want a story. To tell the world the truth about all of you. I know you're good people. I just want to make sure the world sees that."

Kameron held back a sigh. He knew this could be a trick and would log it in, but he was tired and over all of this shit. The humans didn't get to hear the truth. They weren't allowed to know everything. It was for their safety and that of the Pack.

"You know what, man? I'm tired. You know there are avenues if you want to talk to the Pack's publicity team." Yes, they had one now. Like they were some sideshow for the public. He hated it, but he had to play along like a good puppy.

"But—"

"No buts. You're not encroaching on Pack land yet. But

you're close. Go home and get in contact the right way. You're not going to get any answers stalking around the forest, hoping you come across a wolf." The fact that the guy had was because Kameron was having a shitty night. But it wasn't as if this human reporter or truther or whatever the fuck he called himself was going to get any real answers.

There was a script for a reason.

"I want to tell the world who you are."

Kameron let his wolf into his eyes, the gold rim around his irises glowing. The human male didn't back away, but he swallowed hard.

"The world saw who we are. We aren't here for your amusement. You know the laws. Get away from Pack land before you find out what you should be scared of."

Fuck. He hadn't meant to say that, and if this human told anyone, Kameron would be fucked. But he watched as the man drove away, raising a cloud of dust behind him, and Kameron knew he had a problem on his hands.

But first, he needed to clean the leftover blood from earlier off them and get to his family dinner.

He was an asshole, but making his Alpha's mate cry because he didn't show up again wasn't something he wanted to deal with. His brother was meaner than he was, after all.

BY THE TIME Kameron got to his house, showered, and headed to his brother's place, he was over an hour late and knew he was going to get his ass kicked. Yeah, he'd been working and dealing with problem after problem, but at any time during the past two hours, he could have called in one of his reinforcements to deal with the two smaller issues. He hadn't, and now he would be late.

Again.

Of course, as he made his way to the front door, he figured he wasn't the only late one. His cousin Max was skulking right alongside him, his new perpetual scowl on his face.

"You're late," Max said low, not looking at Kameron. From the way his cousin was angled, Kameron couldn't see any of the scars on his face, or the fact that Max had lost his arm in the last battle they'd fought with the humans before everything changed. His cousin had been the nicest one of the lot, the light to Kameron's dark, and now it seemed as if the two of them were vying for position.

"Says the man who's walking in late with me."

"I told them I'd be late dealing with council things. You, on the other hand…"

Kameron rolled his eyes but didn't comment. "What council things? Something I should be aware of?" Max, along with others in their family, was part of the council that connected the Redwoods and the Talons. With so many inter-Pack matings, the council's role had shifted over the past few years. Now, they weren't only working on ensuring that the treaty for the two Packs was solid but also making sure the subtle changes and having two dominant Alphas in a small area under what was almost one large Pack worked and almost seemed normal.

Kameron had no idea how they did it, but since he worked with Gina—the Redwood Enforcer—and Adam—the prior Redwood Enforcer—weekly, he didn't mind the cooperation.

Max shook his head as they walked up the stairs of the porch to the front door. "Just normal business, but we had to start late thanks to one of the member's kids having a birthday. It wasn't a big deal, but yeah, I'm late."

Before Kameron could say anything to that, they were inside and confronted with the sound of every Brentwood family member, including mates, children, and close friends of the family. To say it was loud was an understatement. Max immediately went to a corner, grabbing a beer along the way, and watched the room. Kameron knew that others would go to him soon to talk to him, trying to bring him out of his shell. And, one day, Kameron figured it just might work. At least with the right person—namely, Max's mate. But at least his cousin was trying harder these days by actually showing up to family functions.

Kameron was an asshole, but he didn't have the kind of pain Max did.

"You're late, but I heard you had trouble, so I'll forgive you." His Alpha's mate, his sister-in-law, Brie, cupped his cheek, and he went down to kiss her on the forehead. He wasn't the most emotive, but it was hard not to be with Brie —at least a little bit. The woman had saved his brother, his Pack, and she also happened to be a submissive wolf.

"Long day, but I'm glad I'm here." And as he said it, he knew it was true. Everyone was talking around him, and though he had acute senses, he did his best to block out most of the topics as it would be too much for his wolf to hear at once. But the crowd seemed happy. His niece and future Alpha, Fallon, was in wolf form, being way too cute for her own good and rolling around with Finn and Brynn's daughter Mackenzie, and Ryder and Leah's son Bryson. The adults were watching them while enjoying their evening, and Kameron finally relaxed just a bit.

It was going to be a good night, even if he would rather be at home, trying to forget what he had to deal with that evening.

As soon as he thought that, though, a scent filled his brain, and he held back a growl.

Brie gave him a knowing look, squeezed his forearm, and headed back to Gideon's side.

Kameron hadn't known that Dhani would be there. But, of course she was. She was his brother's mate's best friend and ended up at most functions lately, but that didn't mean he had to like it.

Even if his wolf did.

And, of course, because this was Dhani, and his day had already been hell, she strolled right up to him. She was average height, but that was the last *average* thing about her. Her long, honey-blond hair looked a little darker tonight, but he wasn't sure if she'd dyed it or if it was just because of the waves she'd put in it rather than it being up like usual. She had bright hazel eyes and sharp cheekbones. Her curves were just right, and it made his wolf claw at him.

Damn it.

She scratched her nose, flipping him off, and he held back a smirk. She was constantly finding ways to flip him off, and he had a feeling it was to try and get a rise out of him. It didn't mean that he had to show her he actually liked it.

"Kameron."

"Dhani."

Yes, he was an asshole. But he knew anything having to do with her would be trouble. And he needed to protect his Pack. If he broke that faith by following the mating urge, he'd not only hurt his people, he'd end up hurting Dhani, too.

That's what those of his blood did before him, and that's what he'd end up doing, too.

Since he was now somehow in the corner with her, no one could hear them unless he and Dhani spoke a bit louder. Which was just fine by him since he didn't want to deal with nosy family members.

"Got a minute?" she asked, one hand on her hip, her voice going even lower until it was almost breathy.

His wolf *and* his dick perked up.

Fuck.

"Yeah."

"I know you're my mate—don't open your mouth and say I'm human. I have this knowing. Have since Walker and Aimee fixed the mating bonds. So, yes, I know you're my mate, and that means I'm yours. Why do I know? Who knows, but there it is. When you're ready to do something about it and face up to what you're hiding from, I'll be waiting. What I'll say once you finally fess up...? Well, we'll just have to see."

Then she turned on her heel and sashayed away from him as if she hadn't just rocked his world and fucked up his plans.

Well, shit.

CHAPTER TWO

Dhanielle—call her Dhani—Coburn arched in her sleep, her hands fisted by her sides, but it didn't make the dreams go away. Nothing did but time, and not enough of it had passed for her actions to mean anything but pain.

She'd never been able to make sense of her dreams—at least when she dreamed like this and not hot fantasies of a sexy wolf that didn't give her the time of day. And because she was weird as hell, she always knew when she was dreaming, even if she couldn't wake up. It was as if she were part of the experience that led her to a path she knew was important even if she couldn't understand, rather than dreaming of unicorns and rainbows and, later, maybe constant humping with Kameron.

No, she got the weird.

Because she was the weird.

And she wouldn't wake up until the dream was ready to let go of her.

Each dream was different, even though sometimes it felt as if there were a theme. She drowned in fire. She burned in ice. Every element surrounded her, pulled at her, took her to a new dream, a new level. She'd never been able to make sense of the visions, but she lived them nonetheless.

This one, however, had more than the elements. A woman held a crying child, an infant. Dhani couldn't make out their faces, but she knew there was a desperate kind of love that spoke of something far greater than what she knew and what she could see.

There was a couple holding each other, no fear or angst running through their body language. Instead, there was a sudden joy that Dhani felt even though it couldn't touch the older woman holding the infant. She didn't understand it, but when the flames finally came, and the dream tilted on its axis, the couple wasn't there anymore. The old woman wasn't there either. Instead, a child stared up at her from her own cradled hands. Bright eyes. But there was something missing. Something had been taken from the child.

And she didn't understand it.

Now, she stood in the middle of an empty room, her body draped in white linen, a breeze that seemingly came from nowhere making the dress she wore flutter. Her hair did the same in an unseen wind.

Then the fire came again, and she was no more.

Dhani sat up, her body drenched in sweat, her thin tank top sticking to her skin. She was no longer dreaming, of that she was sure. Because, even in her dreams, she never felt the fear that she did when she woke. She never felt the exhaustion that crept into her bones from her lack of restful sleep. And for some reason, in her dreams, her hair always seemed to be blowing in a wind she couldn't feel. Now, some of her hair stuck to her face in sweaty strands, and the rest was piled on top of her head in a messy bun.

She glanced over at the clock. Since she only had about half an hour before she was due to get up, she got out of bed, turned off her alarm, and decided to start her day. Like usual, there would be no more sleep after a dream like that. She may not have them every night, but they'd come to her often enough throughout her life that she had her own pattern, and her own routine when she needed to deal with the ramifications and the feelings that came after.

Because when she dreamed things like in the one she'd just woken up from, that meant something was going to change for her. It could be small; a tiny thing like a new brand of coffee. Or, it could be life-altering.

To say she was weird was an understatement.

She'd never told her friends about her dreams. She wasn't quite sure how she could start the conversation. Or tell them that it always felt as if she were going crazy when she couldn't really figure out what she was dreaming about or why.

One of her best friends, Dawn, had kept her own secrets, but the fact that Dawn was a wolf shifter and now mated into the Talon Pack seemed a far bigger secret than weird dreams that she might have off and on. Another of their

23

friends, Aimee, had kept the secret that something was wrong with her, that she was dying, from the others. But then again, she'd had her reasons.

Dreams that made no sense and were of no consequence other than perhaps connections to other things in her life didn't seem like something Dhani needed to share. Having her friends know wouldn't change anything except perhaps their perception of her.

She could only wonder what their other friend, Cheyenne, kept from them, as it seemed the four best friends who thought they could tell each other anything, each kept something close to the heart.

With a sigh, she stripped out of her sweaty clothes, tossed them into the hamper, and studied her reflection in the mirror. She didn't like how pale she was and the fear that was in her eyes even though she didn't know what she should be afraid of. She turned to the side and lifted her breast ever so slightly so she could look at the scar that had been on her body since she was a baby. She called it a scar rather than a birthmark because it never felt as if she'd had it since birth. The knowing was just one more thing that made her feel *off*. But it wasn't as if she could explain it.

On her ribcage, right below her breast, was a long scar that looked like a wisp of flame. The mark had grown as she did, and it had forever piqued her curiosity for how she had come to get it. No one could see it unless she wore a very tiny bathing suit, which was something she didn't often do. Or when she was in bed with another. That meant that only a few close people had ever seen her scar other than her parents when she was younger and her doctors.

The red mark didn't hurt, and it didn't do anything. It was just there to remind her every time she looked at herself in the mirror that something was different about her.

Or maybe she'd been spending too much time with one foot in the world of the paranormal that something as innocuous as a scar seemed far more important than just a mark on her flesh.

Of course, thinking about the paranormal made her think of Kam. She couldn't believe she'd actually gone up to him two nights prior and told him flat out that she knew they were mates. She wasn't a wolf, and she wasn't supposed to have that knowledge at all. But then again, that sense of knowing was loud in her mind when it wanted to be. After she had said the words, he had just stood there like a deer in headlights, rather than the wolf that he was. Then she had walked away, a sway in her step as if she hadn't a care in the world. That was so beyond the truth, but she hoped she'd put on a better façade than what was going on in her mind.

She had no idea what she was going to do if he actually came after her and said that, yes, they were mates, and he wanted to do something about it. She also didn't know what she would do if he never came after her at all. What she did know was that she was tired of standing back and waiting.

But the ball was in his court. And she guessed she would just have to wait it out.

She turned away from the mirror and went to get ready

for her day. She had a meeting with the principal before her afternoon classes. She was an elementary school teacher, and that morning was a late start for a half-day for a teacher work day. Normally, she'd be in her classroom, either setting up for the next week, grading papers, or working on lesson plans, but the principal had wanted to see her, and that meant she needed to be on her best behavior.

Most people wouldn't think of her as an elementary school teacher since she seemed to be the more outspoken one of her group of friends. But just because she stood up for those she cared about and herself, didn't mean she couldn't take care of children. She loved teaching, adored enriching lives and watching for that spark when a child truly understood what they were trying to learn. Her job wasn't easy, she worked far too much and got paid way too little, but she still loved almost every moment of it.

But even as she thought that, she couldn't help but wonder if today would be her last day—that sense of knowing coming at her again. She tried to brush it off like she usually did. There was no reason that she wouldn't be a teacher after today. No reason at all. She worked harder than any of the others at her grade level. She was the one they sent the so-called *problem students* to. She didn't think any of her kids were problem students. Some just needed a little extra help or had a different way of learning. That was her job as a teacher, to facilitate what each student needed. Some people didn't understand, but she did, and she wasn't going to stop fighting for her kids anytime soon.

And now she was getting angry and standing on her soapbox for no reason. The principal probably just wanted to talk about her lesson plans or something. The woman was very hands-on, a former teacher herself, even if she was a little standoffish in the personality department. Just because Dhani had dreamed a really weird dream didn't mean it would leach into the rest of her life like it might have in the past.

By the time she had her coffee, did her morning yoga that she really didn't like but needed to do anyway, and got ready for her day, she was still a little early when she got to her classroom. That meant she had a few minutes to make sure that the students' desks were situated and that everything would be ready for them when they returned that afternoon.

When the time for her meeting came, she rolled her shoulders back and did her best not to act as if she were worried when she stepped into the principal's office.

"Shut the door behind you, Ms. Coburn."

Ms. Layne had a stern voice and an even sterner reputation. Dhani wasn't afraid of her, but she wasn't going to lie and say that she wasn't intimidated.

"What was it you wanted to meet with me about?"

"Take a seat."

Dhani did, that sense of dread in her belly tumbling around and growing bigger by the second.

"Ms. Coburn, there's no easy way to say this. But after this meeting, I'm going to ask you to calmly pack up your things and go home. There's a substitute teacher waiting to take over your class. You are no longer needed at the school."

Dhani blinked. "What? What are you talking about? You can't just fire me. I'm a damn good teacher." She probably shouldn't have cursed, but it was too late now, and she was scared—not even angry at this point. The anger would probably show itself soon.

"It's come to my attention, no…it's come to the *board's* attention that you took off too many days in a row last quarter. And while some schools may allow that, we do not. Your personal life seems to have bled into your professional one, and the board is not pleased. *We* are not pleased. There is no union here, Ms. Coburn. There is no recourse for you. If you fight this, it'll be harder for you in the end. I'm sure your *friends* will be able to help you."

Dhani had taken time off to help nurse her friend back to health after Dawn had been hurt. And then she'd done so again when Aimee was hurt. She had used what she thought was accrued vacation time but, apparently, that wasn't how the board wanted to play it. She hadn't missed the way the other woman had emphasized the word *friends* either.

The board wasn't happy that Dhani was friends with the Talons.

And because the new relationship between the humans and the shifters was so fragile, there was no recourse for her. She could fight, she could go to the press, she could try to sue for discrimination, but what would that accomplish?

She'd always been a fighter. Always stood up for others.

And yet, right then, she couldn't think of a reason to fight for her job…but she *could* stand up for what was right.

Stand up.

The words slid into her mind like the dream had, and she did her best to ignore them, not understanding why that sense of knowing would come back with a vengeance now.

"You can't just let me go," she said, her voice growing stronger by the minute.

"Ms. Coburn, this wasn't my decision alone. And, yes, we can just let you go at our discretion. We strive to have teachers who help enrich our students' lives. We cannot have someone here that will keep them in danger. And you having to spend so much time away from the school and with *those* people, tells me you're not putting your students first. You're putting *them* first."

Dhani had heard a lot of prejudiced things in her life. Had witnessed it firsthand and had stood up for those who needed her to do so. She had never been one to back down when someone was in pain because another was misguided or just ignorant or frankly, an asshole. Yet she had never thought the words coming out of this woman's mouth would actually be directed at *her*. What the hell was wrong with people that they didn't want someone who happened to know shifters to teach their children?

Now, she was pissed.

"You're telling me that the board is a bunch of prejudiced assholes that are going to let me go because I happen to be friends with a Pack? That's some bullshit right there."

"Watch your language."

"You're firing me anyway. I might as well do something to make it legit. Because you using some lame excuse that I took too much time off—which we both know is a lie—is just petty. You might as well come out and just say that you're elitist and don't want your precious little humans touched by a wolf. Guess what, I'm human, too. And let me tell you something, honey, the wolves were living amongst us long before you realized you were going to judge them for not being like you, so you can go fuck right off."

She couldn't quite believe she had just said that, but it didn't matter now. She wouldn't have gotten that angry, wouldn't have said what she had if the woman hadn't had such vitriol in her tone about those that Dhani called friends. Because, fuck that shit.

"The parents don't want you here. They're the ones that called, and we agreed that you're not wanted here. Get out of my office. Now. Before I call the police."

"Oh, don't worry. I'm done. But the children that I'm leaving better get the best damn education out there. Because they are the ones you're hurting. Not me." A lie. She hurt so damn badly, but she wasn't going to give this vile woman and her precious board the satisfaction. "And if you try to fuck me getting another job anywhere outside of this school, I'll go to the press. I'll name and shame this damn school. I'll name and shame you personally. I didn't sign a confidentiality agreement, and I won't be quiet when it comes to the way the board is being a bunch of prejudiced assholes."

And with that, Dhani stormed out of the office and past

the other teachers who had totally been listening in. No one would meet her eyes, so she flipped them off on her way out. She was done with this school and the way she'd had to hide who she was so she could *fit in*. She wasn't the calm and demure type. But she had done it for the students.

And now she was being kicked out.

Seething with rage, she went to get her purse out of her desk and froze. Someone had written *wolf lover* and *whore* in red marker on her whiteboard, and now she knew exactly where she stood.

She wasn't wanted. And, apparently, in the school, she had never been wanted.

Just the way Kameron didn't seem to want her.

No, she wasn't going to think about that because she had way too much on her plate to think about a man. She quickly erased the words on the board, the red still peeking through after a single swipe of the eraser. So she sprayed it down and cleaned it again. The words couldn't hurt her any more than that first sight, but she didn't want the students to see. They were young and impressionable, and she was going to miss them with all of her heart.

But she couldn't stay.

So she gathered up her purse, anything personal from the school that was hers, and walked out to her car, ignoring the stares and the whispers. They could talk all they wanted about her, call her a wolf lover or whore, but she didn't care. She was done with this, and she was tired of living between two worlds.

She had spent the past year learning more about the

world of the supernatural than she'd ever thought possible. Now, two of her friends were mated within the Pack, and she spent more of her free time at the den than anywhere else. She wasn't Pack, was only a guest, but now it seemed that she could possibly have a mate of her own within the Pack.

She was so confused; constantly tugged in two directions.

Her parents were human, remote, and distant. Cheyenne was her only human friend left. Dawn had always been a wolf, even though she had hidden it for her own safety. Aimee was now a lion shifter of all things, but no one outside the Pack was allowed to know that. The fact that Dhani did was a huge sign of trust on the Talon's part and one more reason that she didn't understand why she was the way she was. Dhani was pulled toward this new world. She'd always known things, had always listened to her intuition even though she also had a very analytical mind. Her parents had never understood and constantly berated her for it, but she hadn't been able to help it.

She listened to her gut feelings, even though they didn't always make sense. And that was why she had gone off in that office. She had known that morning that something was going to change, but she hadn't been able to figure out what it would be. But as soon as her principal showed her prejudice, Dhani knew that she could no longer work there. She would miss her children more than anything, but that school wasn't the right place for her. And as she drove towards the Talon Pack den, she prayed that there would be a place for her within those wards with the people she trusted most.

She couldn't help but feel like she was on the outside looking in when it came to those at the den, but she had steadily been making friends there over time, and she wanted to be part of something more than herself. She didn't need to be a Pack member, not unless they wanted her to be, and she didn't know how that all worked as a human anyway. But she wanted to be a part of something greater than herself. Maybe she just wanted help. Because she had never felt this lost before, and she didn't know what to do.

She hadn't realized she was crying until she pulled up to the sentry gate and rolled down her window.

"What's wrong, Dhani? Are you hurt?" Tino, one of the main sentries that she usually interacted with and who also happened to report to Kam, leaned into the window to sniff at her. She was still getting used to the way shifters used all of their senses to figure out situations.

Dave, the other sentry on duty, opened her passenger door. She hadn't even known Tino had reached over to unlock it.

"Let us help," Dave said, his voice concerned.

She shook her head, wiping away her tears. "I'm not hurt. "Her voice sounded steady, so she counted that as a win. "I had a really rough morning, and I know I should have called ahead, but I really want to see my friends. Can I come in? Or can they come out to speak to me?"

Tino looked over at Dave, who was now sitting in her

passenger seat, patting her hand as if he were trying to soothe her. They were really great guys, and she was glad they were the two who happened to be here when she drove up.

Tino presumably went to call ahead like she should've done to see if she was allowed into the den. The fact that she'd even been allowed onto the territory at all was because she was familiar to the others on guard duty. But getting into the den itself and passing the wards was a whole other matter. She didn't particularly like going through the wards. Before Aimee had been changed, her friend always had horrible reactions to the magic. Everyone now knew it was because a witch had cursed her, but now that the curse was gone and Aimee was a shifter herself, as well as bonded to the Pack, she had no issues with the wards. Cheyenne had no problem at all—then or now—which said that she was completely human and welcomed into the den by the moon goddess herself.

Dhani on the other hand always got slightly lightheaded, but not as much as Aimee had before everything changed. The others thought it was either because there had been a witch somewhere in Dhani's line, or maybe she was just one of the few humans that were oddly susceptible. Because her parents were both very human and very anti-anything-not-normal for that matter, she had a feeling she was just one of the unlucky few who had adverse reactions to the magic.

That would make what she was about to ask a little tricky, but then again, that sense of knowing was right back at it, filling her brain with impossible dreams.

When Tino gave the go-ahead, she drove past the wards into the side parking lot where guests were allowed to park. As always, the magic tingled over her skin, and she drove really slowly, far below the speed limit in case she got light-headed again. Every time she went through the wards, the reaction was different. This time, she only got a slight headache, but her skin went clammy.

She parked, took a deep breath to shake off the weird reactions, and when she got out of the car, the two people waiting for her were the exact two people she wanted to see. That sense of knowing struck again.

Brie and Dawn stood side by side, worried expressions on their faces, telling Dhani that Tino had called ahead and warned them that she was upset.

Before she could say anything, however, two words slipped into her mind, a whisper in a voice she thought she knew yet couldn't place.

Two words that meant something, though she couldn't help but wonder what.

Stand up.

Stand up?

She'd stood up for herself and her friends at the school, but she knew the words meant something more, something to do with what she was about to ask.

"What's wrong, Dhani?" Brie asked.

"Talk to us," Dawn said. Both were at her side, holding her close.

And because she knew she was loved, protected between these two impossibly strong women who happened to work with the children of the den at the daycare and the school, she did as the words had whispered.

She stood up.

"I got fired today because my former job is full of prejudiced pricks. And because of that, I *knew* I had to come here. I need a job. I want to teach. I know you're short two teachers because of the child boom you had recently, and you have one person getting certified now, but I'm a teacher. A good one. Hire me. I'm not Pack. I'm not a wolf. But I can help. Please, let me help."

She heard the desperation in her voice, knew she sounded as if she were begging, but in the end, that was exactly what she was doing.

Brie's eyes widened as Dawn growled.

"They did what?" Dawn asked.

Dhani explained exactly what the principal had said, but she did her best to let the others know that it wasn't their fault. It couldn't be their fault. Both women growled, their animals in their eyes with that strange glow of theirs as she spoke.

"I need a job. Please, talk to Gideon or whoever approves it, but I know I can help. I already feel like I'm part of something greater than me, and I *know* I have to be here. I can't explain it, but I *know*."

"One of your gut feelings?" Dawn asked, and Dhani nodded. Her friends didn't know about her dreams, but she hadn't been able to hide her uncanny sixth sense after so many years of friendship.

Brie studied her for a moment before a small smile

crossed her face. "Oh, I think we should go talk to my mate now because I know about your intuition, Dhani. And I have a feeling you being here is important."

And just like that, Dhani knew something had shifted within her. She'd done the right thing, had listened to the two words in her mind, and she'd stood up for herself and for her path.

She just hoped it was the right decision in the end. Because it wasn't her fate she was worried about.

It never had been, after all.

CHAPTER THREE

Kameron studied the maps in front of him for what seemed like the thousandth time that afternoon, yet nothing made sense. He'd marked every incursion, every place there had been a boundary crossing issue, but he knew he was missing something. He hated when he had no idea what he was doing, and working with the Aspens—or rather, *against* the Aspens—made him feel that more than usual.

Someone was trying to hurt his Pack, and that meant he was going to do everything he could to protect his people. That was his duty as Enforcer, his duty as a wolf, and yet there was almost a hidden, unseen aspect to what he had to do right then. Because he couldn't fight a ghost, couldn't fight what couldn't be seen, and it made him want to growl or throw something.

And that wouldn't help anyone.

It wouldn't even help his own temper because then he'd just get worked up for nothing. Blade was an egomaniac and an asshole. Kameron had no idea how the man had remained Alpha for so long without his people revolting against him. The man was a dictator, a torturer, and used magic to hurt others, going against all of the rules and values of their people. Magic rebounded on those who used it, it was a base law. And that meant whatever Blade was using to create the magic, created in itself a great sacrifice that he wasn't taking on his own person.

Kam knew what it felt like to live under a dictatorship. After all, his father had been one of the foulest. The former Alpha had abused his power in the worst of ways and almost destroyed the Pack in the end. It had taken sacrifice and going against everything the moon goddess had told him about dominance and hierarchy to survive.

And yet not everybody did. Losing so many to an internal war like that, one they'd survived—if battered, bloody, and broken—had taken a piece of Kameron.

Then the humans had come with their science and technology, with their laws and their fear, and Kameron and his people had lost even more.

And now, here they were, facing a new enemy because it seemed as if his people could never be allowed to live in peace. They would forever be fighting against those who came against them, who wanted what they held within their grasp. And, as Enforcer, he could never stop. Never rest and let go. He always had to be on the front lines, ensuring the safety of his people even if it meant sacrificing his own life and sanity.

Most days, he didn't think of himself as sane anyway. What right did he have to his own sanity when he couldn't protect those that mattered the most to him?

And now he knew he needed to get out of his head because he was sitting in his home office pondering philosophical questions instead of studying the pattern of the rogue attacks like he should be. There had to be a reason so many rogues and demented power users were coming at the Talons in the array they were. He knew it was Blade's fault. *Knew* it from the base of his spine outward.

He knew for a fact that Blade had orchestrated the capture and death of a Central wolf, the kidnapping and torture of the two newest members of the Talon Pack. Somehow, Blade was using the fire witch and her magic to try and take out the defenses of the Talon den, but Kameron had no idea why the fire witch would work with Blade.

Maybe if Kam could think like those who craved evil, he could fight it. But he knew if he followed that path, he would end up lost like his family. His father and uncles had been the worst of the worst, making Blade look like an innocent in comparison. And Kameron knew that blood ran in his veins. He had to be careful, or he could end up like his father. Like his uncles. He didn't know what his brothers and sister thought when it came to the blood that ran in their veins, but Kam knew about his. He knew how controlled he had to be, how icy he had to be to the outside world. He couldn't let emotions override him and turn him into the beast and terror the previous generation had been.

That was why he was obsessed with Blade. Yes, it was an obsession, but if it kept Blade and his ilk away from Kameron's family, he didn't care. If he didn't figure out how the Alpha thought, how he fought, Kameron could lose his family. And he wasn't sure he would be able to survive that loss. They were the light to his darkness, the ones who taught him how to be the wolf he needed to be. He couldn't let them down.

"Why do you look like you're about to throw something at the wall?"

Max's voice pulled Kameron out of his thoughts, and he looked over at his cousin. Max leaned against the doorway, his one good arm folded over his chest so he could look at his nails as if he hadn't a care in the world. Kam knew that wasn't even close to the truth, but if Max wanted to pretend at being the fun-loving cousin again, he wasn't going to stop him. Max grinned at him, but the grin didn't reach his eyes. Kameron's gaze didn't drop down to where Max had pinned up part of his shirt where it only covered emptiness thanks to his cousin losing an arm in battle. He never wanted Max to see pity in his gaze. Frankly, Kam didn't have any. Just anger for those who thought it was okay to hurt those under his care. He knew the scars that covered Max's body were never far from his cousin's mind—not just on his skin, but under it. And Kameron didn't know exactly how to start changing that—and he didn't think it was even his place. But unlike some who treated Max with gentle touches and soft voices because they weren't sure how to bring the Max they knew back, Kam did his best not to change how his cousin acted. Kameron was still going to be an asshole, and Max would still bark back. Only, unlike before, it wouldn't be with laughter. Kam didn't mind, as long as Max still fought.

"I'm trying to think how Blade thinks. So, yeah, I'll probably look like I want to hit or throw things often. Earlier, I thought if I threw something, it might help, but then I'd have to clean it up, and that's not something I'm really in the mood to deal with."

"For a man who likes his house practically Army regulation, you've never been a fan of cleaning." Max didn't move from his position, but his eyes glanced around the room, probably picking up on every minute detail. His cousin was good at that. That's why he'd invited Max over to help him look at the maps and other things. Because Kam was missing something, and he needed a set of fresh eyes.

"If there isn't a mess to begin with, then I don't have to clean it up. That's how things work. You were the one with the messy room growing up if I recall."

"I'm a little better than I was. But I don't see why making the bed every day should be a thing. Just gonna get right back in it later on."

"Yeah, but there's nothing like getting in a nicely made bed after a long day. Or falling face-first into it after a long run."

"That might be true. Why don't you come over every morning and make my bed so I can compare?"

Kameron flipped off his cousin before lifting his chin. "Come take a seat and look at this. I feel like I'm missing something." Max straightened from the doorway and walked slowly to Kameron's side, the ache in the way the other man walked visible even though Kameron knew Max desperately tried to hide it. The rain had been pounding hard all day, and the air pressure had changed suddenly. Even Kameron's bones were starting to hurt from the fluctuations, so he had a feeling Max was in more pain than he let on, not that Kam was going to comment on it. There were lines he didn't cross, and making Max feel like shit was definitely one of them.

"You're probably missing a whole lot since Blade has had years to cover his tracks. The man is so insular that we didn't even know what he held within his den walls. Hell, the man was close enough to help with the human war and fighting the demon back in the day, but he didn't do a damn thing. Instead, he sat back and watched everyone else fight it out while he loaded his coffers and grew the dominant wolves within his ranks."

"I know he's insular, but he's coming out. The Unvieling forced everyone out in different ways. We know that it was the fire witch who attacked our wards and Parker, and that it was at Blade's command. We know that he had Dawn and Aimee kidnapped and tortured. The same with Dawn's friend from her former Pack. We know all that, yet there's nothing we can do about it because, like you said, the Aspens have had a long time to keep their Pack steady. They're stronger than the Talons and the Redwoods combined. And that pisses me off to no end because we are fucking strong. We just don't cross the lines like they do. Because using magic to murder takes a part of your soul away, and that's not something I think our Packs will ever want to sacrifice."

"Damn straight we aren't going to sacrifice our own. And because of that, we need to fight smarter. Let's take a look and see what we can do. I just have a feeling we're not going to be able to fight unless he comes at us again. And I want to see what happens when he throws his worst at us. As strong as we are, I don't know if we're strong enough yet. We're working on it, but the Aspens have had longer to plan, we're just now getting back on our feet."

Kameron sighed at Max's words, knowing they were true. But the fact that they were true didn't necessarily mean he wanted to believe them. The two of them hunched together, going over every attack and slight altercation that might have been the Aspens or they knew for sure had been. Kameron didn't want to miss anything. His brothers and family relied on him to make sure the intel he gave them was solid. He was the Enforcer of the Talon Pack. The bonds that he had with his people alerted him whenever an outside force came against them. And because he had been on a heightened state of alert since the wolves were revealed to the human world during the Unveiling, Kameron was having trouble deciphering what was new and what was something from an older residual threat of intolerance and violence. Because it felt as if the Pack were constantly under scrutiny these days; as if there were outside entities constantly wanting to harm the den. And since it was his job to warn his Alpha and Pack and protect the whole group from those entities, he felt as if he were holding sand with the grains forever slipping through his fingers.

But he wouldn't quit, wouldn't back down. That wasn't what he did, wasn't *who* he was, but it meant that he wouldn't be sleeping well for the time being. That state wasn't new, however, so he'd just get used to it.

CHAPTER FOUR

fter a couple of hours of studying alongside his cousin, Kameron was starving, and Max's stomach was growling so loudly that he could actually hear it. Yes, wolves had heightened senses, but most of them usually ignored things like bodily functions. And because Kam still hadn't gone grocery shopping and didn't have any food in his house, he and Max headed to the center of the den where they had the cafeteria, a couple of cafés, and a newly built farmer's market. It had taken years for their den to feel whole and healthy. Their neighboring Pack, the Redwoods, had a fully functioning town within their den wards, where in reality, they would never have to leave unless they wanted to. The Talons were getting there, albeit slowly. They had spent almost a century falling behind thanks to their previous Alpha and were struggling to catch up. Or at least they had been struggling. With the new blood in the den, the new matings, the new wolves, and now a lion shifter as part of their Pack, things were starting to feel like they should have all those years ago.

With the first rumblings of new laws against wolves being within society and the unknown dangers of what it meant to have the secret of the paranormal out in the world, a lot of the Pack members who lived outside the den were forced to stay within the wards for safety. The wards had buckled and almost disintegrated under the pressure and because of the feelings and betrayals of the past. But now, the wards were stronger than ever, and there was even more space for their Pack to grow. Some members lived outside the den and traveled back and forth as much as they wanted to. Most of them, however, were not in positions of power or out in society, so it was easier to blend in. There was no hiding for Kam since he was the Enforcer and the media knew his face. But he would always have to live within the den wards due to his bonds, so it wasn't as if he could hide out in the human world anyway. Luckily, he loved the land the Pack called home, and though he was shut off from most things, he needed the people around him for his wolf to remain happy.

He and Max were just walking towards the cafeteria to pick up something to eat when Kameron smelled a familiar scent that went straight to his dick. He practically tripped over his own two feet, and stopped in the middle of the walkway, causing Max to bump into him.

"What the hell, man? Is there something wrong? A

threat?" Max looked around them and then relaxed, raising a brow when he caught the scent Kameron had.

Kam shook his head. "No, shit. I didn't realize that Dhani was here visiting the girls." Hearing how those words sounded out loud, he tried to backtrack a bit so Max wouldn't think anything weird. "I mean, shouldn't I be kept apprised of any outsiders within den walls?"

Max gave him a look that said he didn't quite believe him, and Kameron didn't blame him. It was a piss-poor excuse for being so hyper-aware of Dhani's presence.

"She works here now, you idiot, and will be moving in soon. Gideon gave her access to the wards and a small cottage near Dawn and Mitchell's place since she's now working as a teacher at our school. I thought you heard. It only happened yesterday, but it's kind of a big deal. Everyone's been talking about it."

Kam blinked, the roaring in his ears loud as hell. "I've been on patrol, or in my house working. I didn't hear that she moved in. Did Gideon make her Pack?"

He did his best to sound casual, but knew he was failing. Because if she had become Pack without him knowing, that meant she was already too ingrained in his system for him to notice the new bond. Maybe he was fucking up all over the place and was missing more than just the connections to Blade. How the hell was he supposed to avoid Dhani and everything she might mean to him if she was now living practically next door? It wasn't as if he'd known he was consciously avoiding her at first. But now that *he* knew that *she* knew they were potential mates, everything was so damn complicated. Being able to sense a mate used to be the norm for all wolves, then that power went away. Meaning he had met Dhani more than once without feeling that pull towards her. Yeah, he'd found her hot as hell, but he hadn't known she was his mate. And then the mating bonds were fixed thanks to the magic of what Aimee and Walker did in their mating, and Kameron had to deal with the fact that the woman he knew, the woman who kind of scared him on some levels, was his mate.

Not that he'd ever tell Dhani that she scared him.

He had never thought of whom his mate might be. Hadn't pictured a human woman who maybe wasn't quite as human as she seemed. Because if she knew that they were mates, there had to be something else going on with her. He had always told himself he would look for a mate once his Pack was safe. Only it never seemed to be safe. And with Blade out there, his Pack wasn't even close to being where it needed to be, and now he had the one woman that could be his living next door to him.

To say that this was his own version of Hell, a Hell of his own making for that matter, was an understatement.

"She's not Pack. She has a special pass because we need teachers, and she was fired because of her association with the wolves."

Kameron let out a growl, and Max's eyes lit up gold, telling him his wolf was close.

"Apparently, her old boss tried to come up with a different excuse, but they're all just bigots. I don't know if Gideon is going to make her Pack since we've had a few humans become Pack in the past by being blooded in rather than mated, but I don't know the Alpha's plans where that's concerned. All I know is that Brie had a sudden feeling that Dhani needed to be here, which probably means the *moon goddess* wants her to be here, and Gideon hated the fact that she lost her job because of her connection to us. And she's apparently a kickass teacher so, here we are."

Those were the most words he had heard his cousin say in a good long while, and the fact that it was about the one woman Kameron had no idea what to do with, made it just that much stranger. Because he had a feeling Max either knew exactly what was going on between Kameron and Dhani, or guessed and decided not to say anything.

Good, because Kameron had no idea what was going on himself.

"I guess I'll talk to Gideon later so I can keep abreast of the situation. They should have told me." That sounded like an Enforcer and not a growly wolf that wanted to lick and taste the woman in question.

"I guess, but she's not a threat to the Pack. That much we know for sure. But she's here now, and she's coming closer." Max lifted his chin and gestured behind Kameron. "And on that note, I'm gonna go get something to eat, and you can stand here looking like a guppy out of water as she walks towards you."

Max turned on his heel and practically ran, leaving Kameron alone as Dhani walked closer to them. They were off the trail, near to the center of the den but surrounded by trees so they were pretty much alone. Anyone could come up at any moment since this was a high-traffic area, but for now, it was just the two of them.

Kameron really didn't want to be alone with her. Because that meant all he wanted to do was listen to his wolf instead of the logical part of his brain that told him he needed the Pack to be safe before he risked it all and took a mate. His mate wouldn't be safe thanks to his role as Enforcer, and he wanted to prevent that hurt.

But his wolf wanted nothing to do with that twisted logic.

It wanted the woman in front of them.

And because she stood right there, brow raised, he did the one thing he shouldn't.

He kissed her.

He knew he should have asked, should have backed away, should have done anything but what he was doing just then, but he couldn't. He didn't. Instead, he crushed his mouth to hers, savoring her sweet taste as his wolf growled deep in his throat, and Dhani plastered herself against him, her fingers digging into his forearms as she pulled him closer.

He wanted this woman. Had wanted her from the first time he saw her. But he knew this could be a mistake. She could be in danger by mating with him, so he had to stop the kiss.

It was damn hard doing what was right, but he pulled away, leaving them both shaking, their chests heaving.

"What the hell was that?" she gasped.

"A mistake."

Shit. He shouldn't have said that.

Her eyes went wide before narrowing into slits. "Well, fuck you very much." She flipped him off and turned to leave, but he reached out and grabbed her wrist to stop her. Her skin was soft and warm under his touch, and he had to swallow hard not to pull her closer.

"Let go of me, Kam, or I swear to your goddess, we'll figure out what a wolf with no balls looks like when he's part of this Pack. Get me, wolfy?"

He barely resisted the urge to cross his legs. "Shit. I didn't mean that kissing you was a mistake. I meant the timing. I can't be your mate right now, Dhani. It wouldn't be safe." There, he said the words he should have in the first place. "I'm the Enforcer. Lives depend on me. And I'm on the front lines when the battle between the Aspens and us comes about. You'd be in danger if we mated."

The anger leached out of her eyes at his words, but she tilted her head, studying him. "You know? I think that's the most you've ever said to me. You're the quiet guy, Kam. And I've always been okay with that. Because I thought, one day, we could be friends because my friends are your family now. This going from fighting and sometimes talking to a kiss like that? That's not something one can take lightly. I know that the rules of this world are different. I know that once the spark enters and the idea that someone could be your mate takes root, everything changes. But we both know that's not the case for us. The fact that you were honest just now? That means everything. You're afraid you're going to hurt me, you're afraid of what the other

Pack might do. I don't get that, but I can see why you might feel that way."

He ran a hand over his face, annoyed with himself for falling into temptation. She was right, they'd gone from knowing each other on the periphery to him kissing her like he wanted nothing else. It was too fast. Calling it a mistake had made it worse. But he didn't know how to fix it, didn't know if he *should* fix it. Not when he needed to keep her and his people safe.

"I still don't know how you know we're mates."

"I don't know either. But I do. But I can tell you one thing, Kameron Brentwood, just because fate decided something, doesn't mean I have to follow that path. I told you once you figured it out that I'd be there to talk to you about it. But I've watched my friends break before they fell. I've watched my friends fight against what could've been their happiness and almost lose everything because they thought they weren't enough. I don't want to be that, Kam. I don't want to be told I'm not enough. And I know you didn't say that, but never use the word *mistake* when it comes to me again. Whether we learn each other or are ready to walk away, it's going to be both of our choices. Not fate. Not yours alone. Get your head on straight, and then we can talk."

He let out a growl. "I have my head on straight, and it's telling me that I need to put all of my energy into fighting against Blade. And I know that's not the right thing to say, I know that I'm probably going to get burnt to ash if lightning strikes me down for my words, but I wasn't counting on you, Dhani. I never thought I'd find a mate. Not really. And I don't know what I can do about it now. Because as you can tell from that kiss, I want you, but I don't know if I'm the best for you."

Again, he hadn't meant to be so honest, but there was something about the woman in front of him that made him want to bare the truth—and his soul. And he didn't think it was just that they could be mates. He knew he was fighting this against his wolf's wishes. He knew it was probably a mistake, but what if he gave in and she lost her life because of his decisions?

"If the other Pack comes after me, if they come after the Pack, you could get hurt. I don't know if I could forgive myself for that."

She let out a breath and shook her head. "I don't know what to do either. Because, honestly? My life is in a state of flux as it is. Something's coming, something's changing, and I don't know why, but I know it. I don't know why I've always known." She held up a hand when he would have questioned her further. Because, dammit, he wanted to know what she meant by those cryptic words. "One day, I might elaborate on that, but today is not that day. I'm not going anywhere, but then again, neither are you. And there's no rule that says we have to jump into each other's arms right now. One day at a time. Let's just figure out how to live within the same wards, and then the rest will come. Oh, and Kam? That was a damn good kiss."

And with that, she walked the opposite direction, leaving him with a hard-on and a muddled brain. He might think he knew what the right path was for him, but one moment in her presence and everything went out the window. Dhani was a temptation for sure, the only problem was, he wasn't sure he was strong enough to fight that *and* what was to come. Not while keeping her safe.

FACTION

Blade knew what must be done. Rather than worry, he *relished*. It was past time to take this step, and now that he had his top enforcers and witches on his side, he knew he would prevail.

Scarlett prowled around him, the scowl on her face annoying him so he did his best to ignore her. "What's the plan, *Alpha?*"

He hated the way she disrespected the title, but he needed her powers to complete his plans. When she lost her mate thanks to the Talon trash, they'd been forced to form a bond so she wouldn't die since she wasn't nearly immortal like the wolves were. Witches who mated into the Pack were able to lengthen their lifespans by matching them to their shifter mate's. He and Scarlett weren't mates—thank the goddess—but she'd used dark magic to keep herself alive and connected to him, and he hated the oily feeling on his skin thanks to her.

But he needed her, so he would deal with the magic. Once the Talons were taken care of, and she was no longer of use to him, he'd cut the link, and she wouldn't be a problem for him anymore.

"We're going to dispose of the humans that seem to be constantly getting in our way. There are only two left—two associated to the Talons the way they are—but they will be the easiest to get rid of. Then we won't have to waste our manpower taking out their infrastructure. The humans who are slowly coming against certain Packs will do it themselves. Because once wolves start killing humans, the human factions will be happy. It's an excuse to retaliate. But if it falls through, we both know what must be done."

Scarlet nodded as if she had any say in his plans. He hated the woman, but he needed her power. Once the two human women who had latched themselves to the Talons were gone, the other human factions would take care of the den for him. At least that was the goal. Because Plan B wasn't something anyone wanted to see. But he would take care of it. Because there was no other choice.

Sacrifice begets sacrifice, after all.

CHAPTER FIVE

Dhani dreamed again. It didn't matter that she was in a new place, in a different bed, the dreams would always come. She should have learned that long ago, yet for some reason, she had thought perhaps the magic in the wards and the shifters surrounding her would protect her.

But it wasn't to be the case.

Flames surrounded her, licking at her skin, prickling against her soft flesh. She couldn't see through them, but the fact that there was no smoke worried her. Shouldn't there be smoke when there was fire? That was what she'd always learned. But then again, these were dreams, and perhaps this wasn't true fire. Maybe there wasn't truth in anything.

She tried to see, attempted to feel, but all she could sense was the heat of the flames that didn't burn, couldn't turn the world to ash. That would come later. A child cried, and a woman called out, but Dhani couldn't help.

She was never able to help.

The flames parted, and another surge of fire slammed into her—this time, the burning almost real. She screamed.

Then she found herself sitting up in bed, the scream all too real this time, and sweat dampening her skin. She swallowed hard, trying to calm her erratic heartbeat. It wasn't easy when all she wanted to do was wrap herself in a blanket and try not to let vertigo take over. Because she couldn't seem to suck in enough breath.

Then someone slammed what sounded like his or her fist against the door multiple times, and she almost screamed again.

She wasn't in Kansas anymore. Instead, she was in the middle of a wolf den. This time, instead of Dorothy, she was more like Little Red Riding Hood. Or maybe Goldilocks. If Goldilocks had wolves—but she was in and out of beds, so that counted. The loud knock on her door came again, and she got out of bed, wrapping an afghan around her shoulders as she made her way out of her bedroom, through her small living room, and to the door. She looked through the peephole, and though she should have been annoyed; instead, her whole body relaxed at the sight of who was on the other side.

She opened the heavy, oak door, and Kameron walked right in as if he owned the place, his bare chest with its light dusting of hair glistening under the moonlight since he was a tad sweaty. She did her best not to stare at the sweats riding very low on his hips. Very low. The damn man was way too sexy for his own good. No, scratch that, he was way too sexy for *her* good.

"I heard a scream. Are you okay?" His voice was a low growl that went straight to her lady parts. She would *not* cross her legs to relieve the ache.

Her eyes widened, and she could feel her cheeks blush. "You heard me? What were you doing, standing right outside?"

"No, my house is right behind those trees. I'm actually closer to you than Dawn and Mitchell are." His gaze traveled over her body, and she wrapped the afghan around herself a little tighter. She was only wearing a T-shirt and panties, and suddenly, she felt cold. Bare.

She licked her lips, and his gaze followed the movement. "I didn't know that." Someone probably should have warned her, but it wasn't as if anyone knew what was going on—or *not* going on—between them. "But I'm okay. I just had a bad dream." Or a dream that wasn't a dream, but she didn't really know how to tell him that. "I'm sorry I woke you up. I didn't mean to. I didn't know that I screamed that loudly."

He shook his head then ran his hand through his hair. The action brought her attention to his bulging biceps, and she almost swooned. Seriously, swooned. It was going to take all of her energy to resist this man.

"You weren't that loud. I just have more acute senses than most wolves, and definitely better than humans…especially when it comes to you."

"Oh. The whole mating thing?" She didn't know

anything about how any of that worked. And since it seemed so personal, she hadn't asked too many questions when it came to Aimee's and Dawn's matings.

"Yeah. Seems so. As the Enforcer, I've always been able to hear things farther out in the distance than most. Gideon is really the only one who can match me, and he's Alpha. I can usually drown out most sounds since it would be too much for me to function without that ability, but I can't ignore you." He paused, and she was grateful because there was a lot packed into that statement. "You sure you're okay? I know I'm not the best at talking about important things, but if you need to talk about your dream, I can listen. Or I can go wake up one of your friends who would probably be much better at it."

And that was how she knew that this Kameron was going to be far more dangerous than the one who was icy and cold to her. Because she knew that his go-to setting was to tighten his jaw and scare off anyone that could possibly hurt those he loved and protected. But the fact that he was so helpful now, so intuitive? That would be the Kam that could possibly make her think about fate more than she should.

"I'm okay. Really. I have dreams sometimes. Doesn't make for a good bed partner." She snapped her mouth shut and met his gaze. Thankfully, he didn't say anything, but she could see the wolf in his eyes surface at her words. She had to be careful what she said when it came to Kameron, and they were both well aware of that.

"If you're sure. I can check out the house and the surrounding area if you want."

He was such a protector. So much so that he was pushing away anyone that could possibly interfere with that role. Not that she had much to say about it since she would probably do the same in his shoes. Maybe.

"I'm okay," she repeated. "Why don't you go back to your place and get some sleep. I know you have a thousand things on your mind, and you don't need to worry about my nightmares."

"Maybe someone should." And with that, he left her house, not touching her in the slightest, yet she could still feel the heat radiating off his skin. The man was more than dangerous for her, but she knew the pull between them meant something. It was that knowing again, the kind that annoyed her to no end because she didn't know where it came from.

She never knew what any of it meant.

CHAPTER SIX

Thankfully, Dhani's mind let her sleep a few more hours before she was up at dawn and getting ready for her first day of teaching at the shifter school. She couldn't quite believe that she had packed up her entire life and moved in with a Pack of wolves. Well, wolves and one lion. She wasn't used to making such rash decisions, but this one felt right. Gideon and Brie had opened their arms to her in a way she hadn't thought possible. The fact that they had been so open to her not only teaching their young but also living within the den wards made her feel as if she belonged. She'd never quite felt that way when she was outside the den. And that was weird, considering it hadn't been that long ago that she didn't know the paranormal existed at all.

But before she knew that what went bump in the night was truly real, she'd always felt like an outsider. And though she still felt like that somewhat being a human living amongst wolves, it wasn't the same. And maybe that should have worried her, but it didn't.

What concerned her was the fact that Kam apparently lived really close. And he could hear her scream in her sleep. What else could he hear her do?

And that was something she wasn't going to think about because she had a plan for the day. And her plan didn't include thinking about a man. A half-naked man who'd come running to her in the middle of the night.

Her phone rang just as she was about to start her second cup of coffee and look over the lesson plans that one of the maternal dominants had given her. The maternal dominants and Brie ran the show, and Dhani didn't mind. She was in their world now, and as long as she could help, that was all she needed.

But as she looked down at the screen of her phone, she sighed. Because, apparently, the outside world wasn't through with her yet. She picked up on the third ring and tried her best to sound normal.

"Mom, I see you got my message." She loved her parents, she really did. But it was always so awkward with them. She hadn't noticed when she was younger, but she'd always known something was off. They seemed like shells of something they had once been, and she'd never been able to understand what was missing. They loved her, that much she knew. But something was off, and she couldn't put her finger on what. It'd always been that way. They were remote in a way she hadn't been able to understand when she was younger, and truly still didn't now. Because while they had always been there for her, something was lacking. At one point, she had thought it was her, but now she wasn't so sure. Maybe her parents weren't the warm and loving type that she saw in movies, but they had always been there for her in their own unique way.

She just wished she knew what was wrong.

"Of course, we did. I still can't quite believe what I'm hearing, though. You quit your job?"

"No, I was fired. Although, technically, I think I might've walked out before I signed the severance package. It's a little murky whether I quit or was fired at this point. Either way, I'm no longer working at my last place of employment."

"Why on earth would they do that to you? You're an amazing teacher."

It was statements like those that made her heart warm for her family. They truly believed in her, even if they didn't always say things like that.

Dhani wasn't sure if she should tell her mom and dad the truth, but she didn't want to hide things from them. They should know more about her life, even if her connection to them was always remote.

"They didn't like my connection to Dawn." She didn't say anything about Aimee or the rest of the Pack. Because, in essence, her friend was her connection. Dawn telling them that she was a wolf and not a human barista like Dhani had always thought was what had started Dhani's discovery of the supernatural.

"I don't understand."

"They don't like the fact that Dawn's a wolf. Apparently, they figured out that I have more connections to the Talon Pack than they are comfortable with. Which is ridiculous because the Talons haven't done a single thing wrong. The humans started everything. But there was nothing I could do about it in the end. I have a new job, though, so I didn't have to go unemployed for long. Only a couple of hours to be honest."

"I heard in your message." There was a pause. "Is it really safe to be working with the wolves? I know they say they're safe and don't attack humans, but what do we really know about them? I just don't want you hurt. And I don't like the way I sound when I say that."

Dhani didn't either.

She pinched the bridge of her nose. "I'm as safe here as I would be inside any school these days." Probably safer, but she wasn't going to comment on that with her mother just then. She knew her mom was worried because of all of the changes, but she still hated to think that her mom would be scared of those Dhani called friends.

"If you're sure."

She didn't like the uncertainty she heard in her mom's voice, but there was nothing she could do about it. She let her mom talk about what she and her dad were doing for the week, and then she stopped the conversation because she needed to get ready for her day. She hated the fact that her morning had started on that note, but there was nothing she could do about it now. She just needed to go to work, see how she could be this new version of herself, and ignore the things she couldn't change. The fact that those things were starting to pile up hadn't escaped her notice, though.

When she got to the school, Brie and Dawn were already there, waiting for her. Dhani pushed all thoughts of worry out of her mind and smiled at her friends. She wasn't going to lie and say that she wasn't nervous, but she was even more excited.

"I can't wait for you to meet the young ones," Dawn said with a grin. "They're seriously the cutest. Just remember, they're not allowed to shift into their pup forms except for at recess. And yes, baby wolves in their pup forms are just as adorable as you may think. And, sometimes, they let you cuddle them and your ovaries burst."

"That's something I cannot wait for." Dhani grinned just thinking about the babies.

"I happen to think my baby girl is the cutest, and if things work out, you're going to be teaching her soon." Brie hugged Dhani tightly before taking a step back.

As soon as the other woman let go, Dhani knew that this was exactly where she should be. Yes, she was a human amongst wolves, not quite a part of who they were, but not quite out of place either. It was as if she had spent her whole life waiting for this exact moment. She wasn't going to take it for granted. No matter what.

CHAPTER SEVEN

"Is it wrong that I wanted to crawl into the puppy pile and let all of the kids in wolf form crawl all over me?" Dhani asked later when she was at Dawn's house along with Aimee and Cheyenne. Cheyenne had come to the den later that afternoon so she could have dinner with the rest of them. Her friend was now the only one of their group not living within the den wards, but considering that she had a veterinary practice out in the human world, that made sense.

"There is nothing wrong with being enamored with the adorableness that is a wolf in pup form." Aimee smiled widely before taking a sip of her wine. Her friend looked like a completely new woman ever since the curse that had tried to take her life was broken and she'd been turned into a lion shifter. The other woman exuded health and radiance now, and Dhani couldn't be happier for her.

"Since puppies and kittens are my favorite part of the job, I'm going to have to agree with you there." Cheyenne winked, and Dawn threw a piece of bread at her head. Cheyenne caught it easily—the woman had fast reflexes. They were having a fondue party of all things, and the amount of food they'd already consumed was a little insane. Yes, the two shifters were able to eat a lot more, but she was pretty sure she and Cheyenne had almost met them bite for bite.

"You and your need to study us like we're part of your vet practice." Dawn rolled her eyes, and Dhani knew that they were all joking. Although Cheyenne had made a comment or two about how she loved the science behind all the magic surrounding them, Dhani knew that her vet friend didn't think of the wolves—and now cats—as things that might be part of her work.

"Maybe." Cheyenne smiled coyly before dipping the bread she'd caught into the cheese pot.

Dhani tilted her head and looked over at Aimee. "But I guess knowing all of that would be helpful for Walker. Doesn't he have degrees in veterinary medicine? I know he has a few in human medicine since he doesn't want to use all of his strength as a Healer when he could just use science. But what if someone gets hurt in wolf form?"

Aimee nodded. "He has one, but it's been a few years. I think if things ever settle down, he's going to go back and brush up on veterinary medicine. But, yeah, it's easier for him to treat those in the Pack when they're in human form."

She glanced over at Cheyenne. "You never know, he might just ask you to put up your shingle within the den."

Something uneasy flashed over Cheyenne's face, but as Dhani was the only one at a good enough angle to see, she wasn't sure anyone else had noticed. Interesting.

"I think I'm okay with my practice where it is. If Walker ever needs my help, you know I'll be there. But he seems like he can handle most anything. Especially now that he has Leah working with him as a water witch healer by his side. And you as his mate, helping him when you can, as well."

They moved on to another topic of conversation, but Dhani kept her attention on Cheyenne. There was something going on with the other woman that she couldn't quite figure out, but she didn't think it was her place to pry. Considering she had enough on her own plate, she held back from saying anything that could be too intrusive.

"So, are you ever going to tell us about the sexual tension burning between you and Kameron?" Dawn fluttered her eyelashes as if she hadn't just made Dhani choke on her wine.

"What are you talking about?"

Aimee snorted. "Come on, we see the way you two dance around each other. You guys are constantly fighting, flipping each other off, or looking at one another like you want to eat each other up...one tasty morsel at a time."

"It's not like that." She didn't know why she wasn't telling them, but for some reason, she wanted what was going on between her and Kameron to be just between the two of them while they figured it out. She knew she would probably break down soon and tell her best friends what was going on in her mind, but for now, she needed to let her thoughts go in circles for just a little bit longer while she tried to make sense of them.

"What is it like then?" Aimee asked softly.

"It just is. Can we talk about the fact that I caught you and Walker making out beside the cafeteria today? All swoony and totally not secretive at all?"

The girls laughed and, thankfully, let Dhani awkwardly steer the conversation elsewhere. She knew that, one day soon, she would tell them that she and Kam were potential mates. But then she would have to answer the question of how she knew that. And because she didn't have the answer herself, she wanted to wait. And it wasn't as if Kam were ready to jump into a mating anyway. So she would wait.

Just like she'd been waiting all her life.

CHAPTER EIGHT

Kameron did another pull-up, sweat dripping down his brow, and he blinked it away as it tried to get into his eye. He was working himself too hard, and he knew it. But he hadn't been able to sleep the night before with thoughts of Dhani and the secrets she might hold, so now he was working off as much tension he could: stress from the fact that he couldn't figure out Blade's plans; anxiety over constantly being on alert thanks to his bonds as an Enforcer; and the strain that was pure sex and heat that had everything to do with the newest resident of the den.

He let out a growl, his dick hardening at the thought of her, and forced himself to do another pull-up. Then another. If he worked himself to the bone, maybe his dick would be too tired to stay hard all the time.

This was why he needed to stay away from Dhani.

Because the more he was in her presence, the harder it was to ignore what might be between them. No, it wasn't fair to either of them, but she wouldn't be safe as his mate. And the more rationalizing he did, the more he felt like an ass. It wasn't as if she were chomping at the bit to be with him. Instead, they were avoiding each other as if they didn't live so close to one another and didn't work within the same den walls.

He did a few more pull-ups, his body straining, and then went to the ground to start his push-ups. He wore an old pair of sweats and some tennis shoes. But that was it. He hadn't even bothered to put on underwear after his last shift. He'd run as a wolf on his patrol, looking for any evidence that someone had come near the den wards. Thankfully, unlike the other night, everything had been pretty quiet.

There hadn't been another human groupie or reporter wanting to know more about things they didn't understand. And, thankfully, there hadn't been any more rogues coming for them. Though Kam was keeping track of the number of them, they were pretty rare in the grand scheme of things. There were more incursions with fumbling humans than there were with wolves on a tear.

The last major rogue attack that he could think of, beyond the ones that had been sent as distractions, was the one that had made Avery into her wolf. Avery was mated to one of Kameron's triplets, Brandon. She was also mated to a former Redwood Pack member, Parker. That triad had been important to the health of the den and ending the war with the humans. But the fact that his new sister-in-law was now a wolf thanks to a rogue he hadn't been able to stop would always sit heavily on his shoulders.

Yes, Blade had been the one who sent the rogue. And it had been the Aspen Alpha who sent some of the others, as well. But he hadn't sent the one from the European Pack that Kameron had been forced to take care of a few nights before.

Kameron didn't like taking lives. He actually hated it. But if it meant the safety of those he cared about, and possibly ending the pain of the rogue itself, then he would do it. He would be the first line of defense, and hopefully, the last. Because at some point, his Pack needed peace.

And maybe if that peace happened, he'd finally be in the right mindset to be the man that Dhani needed and deserved.

As he tried to push that thought from his mind, his body straining as he continued to do push-ups, a tantalizing scent carried on the wind, and he stiffened in more ways than one.

He couldn't see her, but he could sense her close to the line of trees that stood between his house and her small cottage. She was outside, that much he could tell. He could hear her footsteps on the branches that had fallen from the trees in the windstorm the night before. And he could hear her huff and puff as she carried something into the house.

Interested, though he told himself he shouldn't be, he stood up, rolled his shoulders back to relieve some of the ache there, and then walked past the trees to where he could see her cottage. There, he noticed her lugging boxes in and out of her car towards her house. He didn't know why Mitchell or one of the others wasn't there helping her, but knowing Dhani, she probably hadn't told anyone that she was unpacking more today. He didn't know what she was doing with her old place, but maybe if he weren't such an asshole, he could just ask her and learn more about her life. But he was afraid the more he learned about her, the more he would want her, and the harder it would be to resist her.

There were reasons he wasn't sleeping. And the twisty and curvy thoughts that this woman gave him were just some of them.

"Need any help?"

She turned on her heel at his voice, let out a yelp, and dropped the box she had been holding. Thankfully, she jumped away in time so it didn't fall on her foot. He cursed, not liking the fact that he'd startled her.

"You scared the hell out of me. I know you wolves learn to walk all soft and shit, but if you come up from behind me, can you at least stomp around so I can hear you?"

Kameron's lips tugged into a smile. "I can try, but it kind of defeats the purpose of being an Enforcer."

She huffed out a breath and bent down to pick up the box, but he was faster and picked it up for her.

"Thanks. I think that's just linens, so I don't think I broke anything when I dropped the box. Can you put it in my living room? I didn't have time to label everything like I should have because my landlord kind of kicked me out of my apartment so I'm a little rushed."

He froze, staring at her. "You lost your job *and* got kicked out of your apartment all in the matter of what, less than two weeks?"

"Well, it seems that some of the parents of the kids I used to teach who didn't like me living in my old building. So, instead of giving me extra time on my lease like we had planned so I could move out slowly, the landlord sort of cut everything off early. I know it's more than likely not legal, and it's confusing, and I should probably care more. But I have a new place, and once I can think again, maybe I'll figure out what else I can do within the den or close to it so I'm not leaning on everyone's hospitality so much."

"I don't like that you keep getting hurt because of your connection to us."

"I don't either. But what I hate more is the fact that people are fucking bigots when it comes to shifters."

Kameron growled, this time a little bit louder. "I know it's a lot more political than it sounds on the surface, but if you need us to handle things, we will. It's illegal for them to discriminate against you. Hell, it's illegal for them to discriminate against a wolf."

"We both know that doesn't stop everybody. And maybe I'll be able to fight just a little and help out somebody else in the future. But right now, I need to let my thoughts settle, and for some reason, I feel like I need to be here. And, yes, I know it sounds all woo-woo, but I can't help it. You guys are made of the woo."

That made Kameron smile. "I guess we are. Now, let me help you get the boxes. Because I bet you didn't tell anybody what you were doing today. That way, they couldn't offer to help and make you feel even more beholden to them."

She narrowed her eyes at him. "Not quite sure that I like the fact that you understand me so well."

He wasn't sure either. "You're not going to owe me for this. How's that?"

"Hmm." He wasn't quite sure what that meant, but he noticed that her gaze hadn't left his bare chest for a while. He did his best not to preen because while his wolf wanted her, the man knew this was far more complicated than physical attraction. *Slow*, he reminded himself. They needed to take this at a glacial pace. Or not at all. Because he told himself he couldn't hurt her. And being with him would lead to a world of hurt if anyone found out outside the den. It sucked trying to be rational sometimes.

CHAPTER NINE

Later, Kameron stood with his back against a tree, his attention on the men and women who reported directly to him. He and Mitchell were in charge of training all the wolves inside the den, ensuring that even the submissives were ready to fight in case of an attack. The first job of the submissive wolves was to protect the children and be the last line of defense in case the first line, the dominants and soldiers, were unsuccessful.

Today, however, wasn't for the submissives or even the other dominants that held jobs outside the protective structure. No, this was a training session for his soldiers and the lieutenants who were part of the Alpha's security team. Not all of them were here since some were on patrol at the borders while others were by Gideon's side as Kameron's brother worked, but most were there now, getting their training in so Kameron could ensure that his men and women were ready in case of attack. Gideon would be by soon to check in. The Alpha always made sure he was there for his people, even if it was just to let them know how they were doing and that he *saw* them.

Kameron hated the fact that they had to do this at all since he didn't like the reasons for it. He always trained his people so they were the best at what they did, but the idea that there was a *real* and present reason for this training didn't sit well with him.

Normally, seeing the men and women who'd trained so hard for so long doing well at their positions calmed him somewhat, but he didn't think that would happen today. With a certain woman constantly on his mind, it was hard for him to focus on the good. Because all he wanted to do was ensure that she was safe.

And that was why he knew he needed to be careful. Because if he followed exactly what his wolf wanted, he might end up losing everyone in the process.

"Why do you look like you're going to rip the arms off somebody who makes a mistake today?" Max came up alongside him, his attention on those sparring in front of them, though he spoke directly to Kam.

"I'm not going to rip their arms off." He frowned, narrowing in on one of his men trying to take down his opponent. "Tino, watch that right leg!" he called out to one of his sentries that was working up to soldier level. Tino and his friend, Dave, were working hard to get promoted. Kam would have to talk with Mitchell and Gideon before any decisions were made, though he had a feeling the two would soon be off sentry duty and moved into more leadership-type roles.

Not that sentry duty wasn't just as important—if not *more* important—as some of the longer patrols. Each role was a cog in the system that made up their Pack. Not paying attention to where each person needed to be in order to thrive and keep the Pack safe would go against his position as Enforcer.

"You know, it's not only *your* duty to keep your head down and watch what the Aspens are doing around us. And it's not your fault that they've been able to use darker magic than us to get some of our weakest. Blade *kills* people in order to do what he does. I know they say it takes a village, but it really does take a Pack. That's what the hierarchy is for. We have an Alpha, an Heir, a Beta, an Omega, a Healer, and an Enforcer. Then there're people like me who aren't part of the hierarchy but are still part of this family. I may not have a title, but I'm a damn good councilmember and soldier. Lean on us."

Kameron turned, narrowing his eyes at his cousin. "You sure are talkative lately. Not that I mind, but when you get verbose, I feel like you're up to something." Max had been solemn and silent for far too long. And perhaps since his cousin was leaning on Kam and *his* problems, he wasn't so deep in his own pain that he couldn't find his way out. But Kameron really wasn't in the mood to deal with any extra eyes on him. He had enough to deal with. He didn't want too curious wolves in his business.

"I can go back to being a grouchy asshole if you want. Oh, wait, that's you."

Max turned on his heel, flipping Kameron off along the way, and went to help a couple of the female soldiers who were having issues with their balance. Each of them had given birth recently, only just coming back to training. Their center of gravity was different enough now that it was as if they had to learn from scratch. Since Max had a new center of gravity for a far different reason, his cousin was a good person to help them find their new way.

And if helping others helped Max, Kam would find every member of the Pack who needed help for his cousin.

When Dave pinned Tino to the ground, and Tino yielded, Kam grinned at the look on Dave's face. Tino was usually the better fighter, but Dave seemed to be working twice as hard lately to catch up. The two were Kameron's friends and also happened to be the ones that looked out for Dhani the most when she was on Pack land. Well, maybe not the most since that seemed to be Kameron's role these days, but he wasn't going to think about that too much.

He knew that if he told anyone about his reasons for keeping himself back, it wouldn't make sense to them, but it did to him. He knew the man he needed to be in order to keep those he cared about safe. And though he was attracted to Dhani, and while he knew there might be something more there, he had to weigh all aspects of what could hurt her in the end. Because he didn't know of any Enforcer in any Pack who hadn't lost someone. The Alpha's mate was always protected. It was harder to get to them than any other mate connected to the hierarchy that could be used as a symbol. And that meant that enemies went for the next mate they could get at. And it usually wasn't the Beta. Or the Heir. It was the one they saw as the strongest threat. And that was the Enforcer. The previous Redwood Pack Enforcer had lost his first mate in a horrible way. It'd destroyed the other man, causing such pain and deterioration that Kam didn't know how the guy had survived. But then, decades later, he found another mate, yet he'd almost lost her as well through his own grief and stupidity—and because of the rival Pack who wanted to make her an example.

There were other Enforcers around the country and the world who had lost children, mates, siblings, and even those they were dating. Maybe it was just a coincidence, but Kam didn't believe in those. He trusted in data and threats. And he did not want anyone in his circle to get hurt because Blade or some other enemy saw him as a target. Or saw his mate as a symbol.

And that was just one more reason why he was the icy one of the family. It was not his job to feel. It was not his duty to deal in those emotions, damn it. That was what his brothers—the Healer and the Omega—were for. Walker was the Healer, he had to get under the skin to Heal physical wounds, and by doing so, he connected to the person on a more global level. Brandon, the Omega, literally dealt with emotions and the impact they had on not just the individual but also the den itself.

They were the ones who cared.

Kameron was the one who had to protect.

He didn't need to be a nice guy to keep people alive. Emotions were messy, distracting.

It was better that people feared him. Because then, they would stay safe.

Dhani didn't fear him, yet he feared for her.

And that's why he knew he might need to stay away.

Even if it hurt both of them in the end.

CHAPTER TEN

Although Dhani had always known that living within the den would be different than the life she was used to, she hadn't quite expected the dramatic changes her life would undergo after she moved into her small cottage and started working with the young wolves of the den.

Instead of being completely structured with what she had to wear and what she had to say, she could wear jeans and a T-shirt and be completely comfortable. Not that she actually would wear jeans to teach…because there were just some lines she wasn't sure she could cross—even if it was all in her head. But she did wear cute leggings and flowy tops so she was comfortable while still looking somewhat presentable.

The lesson plans were given to her, but she was also able to tailor them to each student in need. The den's school was much smaller than her old one, so she only had twelve students in her class. Apparently, that was a huge boom compared to the previous years since there were some gaps in the children's ages. That meant there were some grades in school with *no* children yet, but she was told that was changing.

She was learning so much about shifters that she knew she would probably never be able to remember it all. For instance, many mated couples had way more than one or two children like humans did. In fact, a lot of them had eight or nine. Considering how many siblings Kam had, that made sense. Twins and multiples were not uncommon, either. In fact, they were more common than singles in some family trees.

And because shifters were so long-lived, they tended to have all of their children in one big burst over one or two decades. That way, all of the babies could grow up together as true siblings rather than being somewhat disconnected because of such large age gaps. She'd always wondered why some mated couples could live into their three hundreds or more, but all of their children were around the same age. She would've thought maybe they would spread their kids out a bit more, but it made way more sense the way they did things. Sometimes, there was a happy accident later on in life. Much later in some cases, since she knew of one family that'd had their youngest a hundred years after they had their other children.

And then, sometimes, the couple had the sudden urge to have another baby even if it was fifty years after their others. There weren't set rules, but most of them went with the grain instead of against it.

However, up until recently, at least within recent memory of the den, there hadn't been many children born to the Pack. There weren't many mated pairs either. She didn't know everything behind that pain, but she knew it must run deep. It wasn't her place to ask all the questions and learn all the history without being invited in. She knew she wasn't Pack, even though she was a friend to them. And though she should perhaps feel a little more disconnected than she did...she didn't. Maybe it was because she was finding her own way rather than waiting for others to invite her in. Before, when she was in the human world, she'd always been the one waiting. Only her best friends, Dawn, Aimee, and Cheyenne, had been able to keep her close, and keep her grounded.

Dhani shook off those weird thoughts and went back to thinking about the children she worked with daily. They had brilliant, inquisitive minds. And while she truly missed her previous students, she knew she was right where she needed to be. Learning to teach shifters was a whole other matter. Sometimes, they would shift unexpectedly and be embarrassed. Then she had to help them shift back and straighten their clothing. Because a little wolf pup caught and tangled in their clothes was scary for the youngster.

And then there was the growling, yipping, and other things that went with being the only human in a room full of shifters.

On top of that, not every child was just a wolf. Some

were children of witch and wolf pairings. Meaning, she also had to be aware if any child got a little too excited and used their elemental magic. There hadn't been an issue yet, but Dawn had warned her to be on the lookout. There were always witches nearby to help in case of an incident or emergency, though. Dhani was never alone, and there were always others around to help her with any of the paranormal aspects that were a little out of her depth.

It also made her think about the fact that, yes, she was the only true human around. Everyone around her had more strength. Some had special powers, and many of them were a full century older than she was. She didn't feel out of place, but she was aware of her humanity.

Maybe that was why Kam wanted to stay away from her.

No, she immediately pushed that thought out of her head. He had said that he wanted her, but he also wanted to protect her. While she understood that, she also didn't know if she wanted to pursue a relationship with *him*. Because relationships in this case were worth more than a single night. They were permanent. They *meant* something. Mating was for life. It was serious. If she could take it as slow as possible, she would.

But if she let herself think beyond the idea of her relationship, she then thought of whom she could be within the Pack itself. Could she see herself as a wolf? She didn't know if that was for her—or Cheyenne for that matter. Because two of their four were already moving on with their lives. What did that mean for her and Cheyenne? Dawn and Aimee were each shifters, practically immortal, and would one day leave Dhani and Cheyenne behind. Unless Dhani became a wolf.

But was that for her? Could she see herself fighting another soul, another form of dominance within her body as she tried to figure out who she was before and after that point in time? She wasn't sure, but she knew it was a much harder question than thinking that magic and shifters were cool. Because while that was the case, she could see the challenges evident in each of her children as they wrestled with their own wolves and magic. They were so strong, yet they couldn't be like the human children she'd taught before. They couldn't grow up as she had as a child.

The point might be moot, however. Because with the new laws in session thanks to humans wanting to control the shifters any way they could, wolves could not change humans into one of them even under special circumstances. It had to be through a mating bond. If a shifter found their mate out in the human world, they could change that person into one of their own. And though there were ways to get around that, they were all dire circumstances that Dhani didn't even know the details of. And even if, for some reason, she found herself wanting to be a wolf, it didn't mean that the others would allow her to be Pack. There was a difference between being a guest and being family.

Yet if she were to mate with Kam, in order for her to live her life with him into eternity rather than her normal life-span, she would have to be changed. Only witches could remain in their original forms through a mating bond.

Apparently, that magic allowed them to match their lifespans to their mate's.

Humans didn't have that option.

She thought that was kind of crap since she loved being human. Sure, she loved her friends that were shifters and witches, but she loved herself, too.

If she were to allow herself to mate Kameron, let herself be in a relationship that was more than a single date, one that stretched into eternity and bonded her soul to another, she would have to leave part of her life—a part of herself —behind.

And while she had already done that somewhat when she took the job here, it wasn't the same as completely altering her life and the way she lived for someone else. Some might say she would be altering it for herself, as well, but since she wasn't ready for that, she couldn't truly think about it.

As she sat on her tiny porch swing, she let all those complicated thoughts wash over her. Yes, she was exactly where she needed to be, but finding the next path and taking the next step, that was as murky as ever.

She was going to have dinner with Brie and her mate, the Alpha, later tonight. Gideon wanted to get to know her more since she was now living with his Pack, and she didn't mind. She liked him, and though he looked like Kameron, she still found her man far more attractive.

She paused, taking a few mental steps back on that train of thought. *Her man?* Since when had she started thinking of Kameron as her man? She needed to get a grip because if she didn't, she might make a mistake and go too far, too fast, and regret it in the end. And she didn't want to live with regrets. She knew Kameron was the same way.

As if she'd conjured him from thin air, he was suddenly standing in front of her, a curious expression on his face.

"What are you thinking about so hard that you keep frowning?"

He smelled so good, and she had no idea why she thought that. She watched his jaw clench as he studied her, but she didn't think it was in anger. It only meant that he was thinking...and looking damn sexy while doing it.

She wasn't about to tell him everything, but she could at least tell him some. "I was just thinking about how complicated it is in a world that isn't just humans with their own wars and issues. But, really, I'm just thinking about the fact that I have dinner tonight with Gideon and Brie. They said not to bring anything other than myself, and now I'm worried about that."

He moved so he was a bit closer, and she swallowed hard.

"That's a lot to worry about. But they're not going to mind if you don't come with anything. Brie is submissive, and though you know the word, the reality of it is deeper than what most think. It means she needs to take care of everybody that she calls her own. She will feed you all the food that she can, and the house will be warm, inviting, the candles lit, and Fallon, the baby, will crawl all over you and make you smile. Gideon will glare and growl, and then will probably laugh at something stupid, and you'll know that you fit right in. It's how those two work."

She smiled at that. "I kind of like that idea. I hope it works out like that. I'm still nervous. If I think about the fact that I'm going into an Alpha couple's home, I'll start to panic. Yes, I've been there before, but never alone. And sure, Gideon's a great guy, but he's still the Alpha of a Pack of shifters. I've no idea how my life ended up like this, but I'm trying to catch up."

Kameron moved forward so he was leaning against the railing of her porch, so close to her on the porch swing that she could feel the heat of him. The man was always so hot—literally and figuratively—that he heated her from the inside and out anytime he was near.

"I was just on my way home, by the way. I found myself walking past your place instead of going around. I hope it's okay that I'm here."

She swallowed hard. "I didn't want to ask. What are we doing, Kameron? Because if we aren't careful, we're going to hurt more than each other. I'm not a fan of uncertainty, but I don't feel like it's time yet to make any decisions."

He shook his head, stuffing his hands into his pockets. "We have time. But the reasons I stated before haven't changed. I'm going to hate myself every day for having to push you like I was forced to. And I guess you were right earlier; I don't have my head on straight. Because I don't know what I'm doing either. And I can't be that man. I can't be the fumbling guy who makes mistakes. People count on me. And I don't like that I don't know what I'm doing."

She gave him a soft smile, knowing that they were both on the same page, even if that page didn't make any sense and would probably hurt them both in the end.

"I'm not asking for promises. I know you aren't either. But, Kameron? If and when the time comes when promises are made, then those are the kind that are never broken. I'm not that person. You can't just walk away once I give in. So go back to your house. Go be the hero that I know you can be, the hero that you need to be. And I'm going to try and find my place here. I'm going to try and figure out this new me. And then, maybe…maybe we can figure out if those two can fit."

Thankfully, Kam didn't say anything after that. Instead, he leaned forward, brushed his knuckle along her jaw, and then walked away. She sat there on the porch for little bit longer, relishing the feel of his touch, even though it was only an echo now.

Could she be a mate? Could she let herself fall and be a new person in this new world? Because while she felt the pull, and she knew they could be mates, she wanted to know if he was hers in truth. She wanted to feel that emotion, she wanted to love.

She wanted to *be* loved.

Because she was still human, after all.

SNATCHED

Blade sat on the soft couch in front of the two humans as he explained to them the horrors that awaited their daughter. He did his best to sound sympathetic. He wasn't a compassionate man, wasn't sure he'd ever felt anything close to an emotion such as that, but he knew how to fake it when it counted.

The two in front of him held each other close as he explained that their daughter had been kidnapped and that the only hope for her life was to do the unthinkable. He told them that he would make the connections, get the plans in place, and that he would do all in his power to protect their precious baby girl.

And all the while, they had no idea that the true wolf, the true Alpha was the one in a suit with a soft smile and kind eyes.

At least, he hoped they were kind. Because he wasn't a benevolent man.

But he would lie to get what he wanted.

He would kill to get what he desired.

And now, he would use those that would come up against him to get what he deserved.

Because this couple in front of him would do exactly what he wanted. They would say exactly what he told them to. He would coach them so they took the next step to bringing down the Talons.

And if their daughter died along the way, so much the better. Because then she would be out of his life, no longer a symbol of what the Talons could have. Then, the human factions who were against the shifters would do their duty and take out those who dared stand in Blade's way.

Because he was the Alpha that mattered. He was the wolf that would rule all.

And the humans would one day know his wrath.

But for now, they had no clue.

For the time being, they would learn to fear the Talons. Until his plan was set in motion.

CHAPTER ELEVEN

K ameron ran a hand over his face, exhausted after another long night of not enough sleep and a full day of scheduling and patrols. Max and Mitchell had been on training duty for most of the day, and that meant it was his job to plug any gaps that might come from having so many of his soldiers brushing up on their evaluations and training. He normally wouldn't have minded it, but the lack of sleep and how hard he'd been pushing himself recently was almost a little too much at this point.

He was then perhaps thankful that there was a Brentwood family dinner tonight at Gideon and Brie's. Or maybe he wasn't as thankful as he needed to be, but he knew the time together was needed. With so many new babies and matings within the family, they tried to keep the dinners to at least twice a month now so everyone could catch up with each other, but as one of the only two non-mated Brent-woods left, it was a lot of family all at once.

And it probably didn't help matters that he'd heard they invited Dhani to the dinner so she wouldn't be alone in her cottage all night with all her friends—minus Cheyenne, who was spending less and less time in the den.

That meant he'd have a whole evening surrounded by his too curious family who all tended to see too much when they tried, and the one woman whose scent constantly sent him over the edge to oblivion where he had to use all his control not to mark her as his right then and there.

But he had to go. The family didn't let Max get out of these functions, and Max had a legitimate excuse to skip them, so Kameron didn't have a chance. They were pack animals at heart, and that meant being near one another was what their wolves needed. They *liked* it, even if their human halves sometimes wanted space. Lone wolves could get by with long stretches of time away from one another, but even they needed some interaction.

And even though some might think the opposite, Kam wasn't a lone wolf.

That meant that his wolf would actually enjoy the dinner tonight even if Kameron would rather be anywhere else. He loved his family, but he needed time to think about Dhani and what they were going to do about this burning need between them that was nothing so mundane as normal lust. And he couldn't do that when she was so close to him.

But he wouldn't have a choice at the proximity, it seemed. As soon as he walked into his Alpha's house, it was chaos once again—family, food, and a sense of what should have been rather than what Kam had been dealing with in his head for weeks.

Gideon and Brie were snuggling with Fallon, the two looking as if they'd mated last week rather than a few years ago. Finn and Brynn were standing near them, talking and snuggling each other. They'd left Mac over with the Redwoods tonight so Finn's parents could play grandparent and spoil the baby, at least according to what Brynn had said before she came.

Ryder and Leah were on the couch with Bram, Shane, and Charlotte. The latter triad wasn't related to the Brentwoods, but they were practically family since Shane was one of Gideon's lieutenants, and Charlotte was Finn's and Parker's cousin. Everyone was so interconnected these days, it was hard to keep the wolves straight.

Kameron didn't know what the group was talking about, but the normally stern guys were laughing up a storm, and the women were rolling their eyes. Ryder and Leah's son was draped over Ryder's lap, sleeping away despite the noise.

Brie had laid out appetizers for everyone, and Mitchell and Dawn were at the dining room table, talking with Brandon, Avery, and Parker. Every once in a while, Parker would whisper something into Brandon's and then Avery's ears that made them both blush, so Kam had a feeling the triad wouldn't be staying long after dinner.

Walker and Aimee were standing in a corner, his brother's head bent low as he listened to his mate's soft voice.

Walker had his hand on Aimee's waist, the other playing with her hair. The two looked as if they thought they were the only ones in the room, and in their world, that may have been the case.

Kameron's gaze had gone to the opposite corner before he walked all the way into the house, but he'd done his best to ignore it as Max and Dhani were standing side by side, surveying the house as they had a low conversation. Kam's wolf bucked, wanting to tear Dhani away from Max's side, but he wasn't going to be jealous of the fact that his cousin could so easily talk with Dhani. The problem with Kam and Dhani wasn't that they couldn't have a conversation. No, the problem was that they wanted to do *more* than talk, and neither of them was prepared for the consequences of that.

Kameron had walked in late, again, because he'd been avoiding being in the same room as the woman who held the scent that made his wolf crave her more than he ever thought possible. The mating urge rode him hard, and he did his best not to heed it because if he did, there would be no going back, and she'd be in more danger than she already was by being associated with the Talons.

Before he could go over to one of the groups and make conversation as his Alpha's mate would want him to, he noticed the TV screen. It was muted, but what he saw made him freeze.

"Shit," he mumbled, moving forward to turn up the volume. The others in the room stopped their conversations as he did. They all knew he wouldn't have turned it up if there weren't a reason—he was an asshole, but not a rude one.

Dhani immediately came to his side and slid her hand into his as the news anchor started talking. He ignored the others as he felt their stares, knowing that what was on the TV in front of them changed everything and was far more important than what the others saw between Dhani and him.

"We're going back to Jack, where the story is unfolding. We'll have more information soon."

Jack, the reporter who stood next to a pale, older couple, looked stern but familiar.

"Fuck."

"What?" Gideon asked from his other side. Dhani shook next to Kameron, her scent shifting to fear, and he had a bad feeling…even worse than before.

"That's the reporter who came to the den looking for answers. Hell. And the woman behind him not saying anything is the damn woman who called herself a groupie. Who knows what we missed before I turned up the volume, but this isn't good."

"Whatever happens, it's not your fault," Brie put in. "You were doing your job."

"Not good enough, apparently."

"It won't be his fault," Dhani said, her voice hoarse.

"Oh God," Aimee and Dawn said together as they came closer.

"Is that…?" Dawn asked.

"Yes," Dhani said, her body shaking even more next to

his. He didn't move to put his arm around her, but he did squeeze her hand. "Those are my parents. *Why* are my parents on TV?"

"Fuck," Gideon growled. "This is going to be bad."

Beside them, Shane was on the phone talking to the others on his team, and Kameron knew they were making sure the den was safe. Kameron's team would be doing the same, and once he had all the facts, he'd make some calls of his own.

Jack began speaking. "We're here outside the Talon den area, begging for the truth. We know what the government tells us, but I've seen firsthand what terrors those who push us away can bring."

Dhani's mother whimpered, and Kam growled, squeezing Dhani's hand again.

"These wolves are scary, insular, and perhaps even murderous. As we learned before, they pushed away poor Jesse, who now stands behind us. They forced her to walk alone in the forest, lost and near death."

"Lies," Kameron growled.

"We know," Brandon said. Kam could feel Brandon trying to soothe the emotions in the room since he was the Omega and that was his duty, but Kam never let Brandon close enough for it to work on him.

"I was threatened with horrendous things for wanting to know the truth. And now we're here with the Coburns. They've come to beg for their daughter's life. And I just want to emphasize the danger that could come from this single broadcast. We are risking our lives for the truth and to save a young woman's life. Mr. Coburn, tell us what happened."

Dhani's father pressed his lips together before giving a tight nod. "Our daughter has been kidnapped by the Talons. She's a *normal* human, and now she's being forced to live within their wolf den and do God knows what. If it wasn't for Mr. Aspen, we wouldn't have known that our Dhanielle had been taken from her home."

"Blade," Kameron hissed out. "Fucking Blade *Aspen*. Real smooth, asshole." Blade didn't have a last name, so using Aspen was just a fuck you to Kameron and his Pack.

"These wolves forced Dhani out of a job. Her nice job where she was making a difference. They made it impossible for her to work there. They made it dangerous. And now, we can't talk to our daughter. We can't see her."

Tears streamed down Dhani's mother's face, and while Kameron wanted to take Dhani away from this and protect her, he had a feeling her parents *believed* what they were saying. If Blade were involved, this was beyond surface deep. Something else was brewing.

"We just want our baby girl back," Dhani's father said, his voice choked up.

Jack gave them a solemn nod. "We've reached out to the Talons but have heard nothing."

"Lies," Kam growled out once again. "Fucking lies."

"We've also reached out to local authorities, who said they would look into the matter. Dhanielle Coburn has been kidnapped and will most likely be forced to do unspeakable things. If the wolves turn her, they will be breaking the law.

She is not under Pack jurisdiction, but bound by human laws. The wolves must see this. We cannot let them win."

The news went on to other things, speakers discussing the impact of the kidnapping and what could happen if this got out of control with even more broken laws. Kameron was sick to his stomach. When he looked down at Dhani, she was pale as a ghost, her body shaking.

"Shit," he whispered, tugging her close. "I'm so damn sorry."

"No. I am," she gasped out. "I can't believe...those were my parents, but they weren't. You know. I mean, I just talked to them, and they sounded fine."

"They looked hexed," Leah said softly from behind them, and everyone turned to look at the water witch. "If Blade is involved, then so is his witch, and I have a feeling he used her to make your parents do what he needed them to. To see what he needed them to see."

"I can't believe they would do this." Dhani pulled away from him, wrapping her arms around her middle. "I mean, I know they've been growing even more distant and they weren't answering my calls, but I didn't think twice about it. I just thought it was normal. How things went after a time where we didn't have much to talk about. I didn't realize there would be an egomaniac Alpha wolf convincing them that I was kidnapped. Perhaps even hexing them into going on national television. I'm so sorry. What can I do? I can go. I can tell people that you guys have been nothing but kind to me and would never do anything like that. Would it matter? That reporter seemed predisposed to the idea that you guys did this. I'm just so sorry."

Kameron didn't touch her, but his wolf wanted him to.

He wasn't sure what he was going to say, but before he could even open his mouth, Gideon spoke instead. "We know this isn't your fault. It was bound to happen. The more things start to settle, the more those on the fringes find ways to speak. I'm worried if you go on television now, they're not going to believe you. Because you're still out of our jurisdiction, just like that journalist said. If the authorities truly do come here like they were saying, we may not have any recourse to let you stay. But we can't allow others to force our hands. The lines are blurred at this point, and we're just trying to keep things settled in this new world. You may be employed here, but in the eyes of the humans, you're still one of them. And I can't make you Pack by changing you. It's against the law, and maybe we could've found a way around that before, but there's no way now. We're under too much scrutiny."

Kameron's claws pressed under his skin, his fingertips burning, but he held them back—barely. He knew he should say something to Dhani, but there wasn't that kind of time, and frankly, he didn't know what he would have said anyway. "If you perform a mating ceremony, then she's Pack, right? Then the humans can't do anything."

A few gasped, while the others looked at him with pitying glances. His eyes were only for Dhani, though. Because he had just outed their secret, the one they'd both held close to the vest because it had been about the two of them, not about anyone else. And now, those closest to them knew, and he just hoped it was enough. Because despite the ramifications, he would mark her right there, get the blessing from his Alpha, and take her to his place to complete the mating bond. He'd be damned if he let her or his Pack get hurt because of his actions.

"That almost sounds a little too convenient," Gideon began, but held up his hands when Kam growled. "I'm not saying it's not true. I had a feeling there was something going on between you two, but I was doing my best to ignore it because, while I'm the Alpha, I do try to stay out of everyone's business—don't snort, Mitchell. But what I'm saying is, it might sound too convenient for the humans. We have no way of proving mating bonds, no way of saying that she's Pack without it sounding as if we're scrambling. And, frankly, I haven't heard a word from Dhani saying that this is something she wants. It takes two—or three in some cases —to mate. Not just the desire of one."

Dhani raised her chin and met Gideon's gaze for a moment before she turned to Kameron. "What if we play Blade's game? What if we televise the mating ceremony? I'm not talking about the actual bonding, but what if we give them something that looks like a wedding, something that humans will understand. I know it's not exactly what you guys do, and I don't even know if it will work, but if it's what we need to try, then I'm game. Because I'm not letting my family hurt *this* family."

The others started talking around them, making plans and pretty much agreeing with what he and Dhani had just come up with. But the only two people not speaking were him, and the woman who would officially be his mate. Soon.

He knew they needed to talk, but it looked as if they weren't going to bother at that point because they were both going to do this for the good of their people, the good of their Pack.

And he'd never hated himself more than at that moment. Maybe if he had stopped that reporter, maybe if he had listened, this would be different. Maybe if he had listened to what Jesse, that so-called groupie, had wanted, things would be different. Maybe if he had found Blade and ended things before they truly began, things would be different.

Maybe if he hadn't been so closed-off, and hadn't been such an asshole, things would be different.

Because now, he was pushing a woman into mating, forcing a bond that both of them said they could feel the need for but hadn't said they wanted.

And now they were doing the most taboo thing possible by playing Blade's game and having their mating televised.

In the end, he would end up with a mate, one with a bullseye on her back because of his actions.

There was a special place in Hell for him, and it looked as if he were already living in it.

CHAPTER TWELVE

When Dhani was a little girl, she had played wedding games like most of her friends. She had married three or four of her friends over time, using pillowcases and parts of lace tablecloths as veils. She had used dandelions and white daisies as her bouquet. She had danced to soft songs with her teddy bears as she imagined her perfect wedding day.

The image had changed over time because while she'd had a few serious relationships, none of them had ever screamed *marriage* to her.

She'd been too busy and had never found the right person for her.

Now it seemed that nothing from her childhood would actually come true.

Instead of lace and daisies, she was going to mate—not marry—a man she was just starting to know...under duress.

He had said straight to her face that he didn't really want to want her. He may not have used those exact words, but she knew the undercurrents. He wanted to keep her safe, and despite the burning heat between them, she understood. But now it seemed that, no matter what, she couldn't truly stay safe.

And yet it wasn't her safety that she was thinking about when she agreed to a televised mating ceremony. It was the safety of the new pups that she taught, the safety of her friends that were connected to the Talons. She knew that Kam would do everything he could to protect her, and maybe one day when she was a wolf, she would have the strength to protect herself. Now, she was giving up the idea of doing something just for her, falling for someone and letting go of the consequences. Now, she was doing something for the good of her people, or at least the good of the people who had taken her in and held her close to their hearts.

Nothing was as it should be. She should have been standing with her parents, crying soft tears as her daddy gave her away. Her parents would not be attending this farce. They would see it on television like the rest of the world. And while she feared for their safety because Blade had evidently been near them at some point, she couldn't let her parents close to the Talons either. Gideon had sent a couple of soldiers out there to watch over her parents, but in secret. Because they had no idea if Blade was still around or if he'd left some of his men to keep an eye out.

It was a dangerous game, and she hated that her parents

had become part of it. Because as much as things had gone wrong between the three of them, she couldn't believe that they would go to the extremes they had. The idea Leah had mentioned when she said that they looked hexed had been an oddly soothing reaction, even though it should've felt horrendous. She should have been horrified that magic had touched her parents. Conflicted was such a small word to describe what she was feeling.

Dhani should have been spending her time trying to figure out who would be her maid of honor out of her three friends. Instead, Cheyenne wouldn't even be there. Her friend had wanted to come, but the others had said it would be too dangerous for her to be truly connected to the Talons out in the open like that. They all knew that Blade knew that Cheyenne was part of the Fearsome Foursome of friends that were now connected to the Talons, but they didn't want the rest of the world figuring out the details. So, once again, their friend was excluded and on the outside looking in. But with mating ceremonies between wolves, there weren't maids of honor or bridesmaids. Dawn and Aimee would be standing with their mates, looking on, but Dhani didn't know if she would feel any pride or joy radiating from them like she might have if things were different. Because she didn't even know what she felt for Kam. How were her best friends supposed to? She had a feeling that both of them were a little hurt that she hadn't mentioned that she could feel the mating pull when it came to Kam, but there hadn't been time to talk about it.

She figured there would be time once the dust settled

and she found herself mated to a man who didn't want to mate with her...or rather one who was so protective that he was afraid a mating might make things worse. But then she didn't know what kind of person she would be at that point. Gideon had said she would be Pack, but she wouldn't be a wolf. Not right away. She would be a mate, a Pack member, someone who had been a public source of pain and fear for the den. How was she supposed to face herself in the mirror while all she could think about was the pups that could be in danger because she had thought her place was with the Talons?

They weren't going to have their mating ceremony within the den circle where almost all other ceremonies were held. This would be on Pack territory, but not within the wards.

Gideon would say some of the same words he would during a normal ceremony, but not all of them. Those were personal and were part of the Pack's history. Some things were not meant to be in the public eye. She wouldn't be Pack until she went back to Kameron's house, and he marked her. And then they would make love. By binding those two parts of themselves, the wolf with the mark, the human with the spilling of seed, the mating bond would snap into place. And once that happened, she would officially be part of the Pack.

There were other ways to become part of the Pack, but all of them included Gideon and blood—something not in line with what the humans would allow. That wasn't something they would put on television. Instead, they were going to give a show. Broadcast a pleasant mating ceremony that was basically a fake wedding, and she would show the world that she was happy where she was and that she was in no danger.

Somehow, Ryder and Max had figured out exactly who to talk to in order to set everything up. They would be taking no questions, there would be no statements beyond the original press release they had just put out, but they had explained that Dhani would soon be a Talon member through mating. She knew not everyone would believe it, but maybe if they saw the ceremony, they would start to. Once she was Pack, once she was a mate, then she would be safe, and she would be able to keep the Pack safe.

At least, that's what she hoped.

She couldn't help but feel as if she were drowning, perhaps swimming in circles and not able to tread water. They were going about this all backwards, and she knew she might be making a mistake. But that was the only mistake she could make. The mistake she needed to.

Perhaps one of the strangest things about all of this was that she and Kameron hadn't even really spoken. They had talked to others about what they needed to do, but they hadn't spoken to each other. The broadcast had aired the day before, and they were already working on the makeshift ceremony that would happen that afternoon. Kameron had given her a look, said he would talk to her later, and then he left with Gideon to ensure that the den was safe in case this was just a distraction so Blade could mount an attack.

The thing was, she totally understood that. All of this did

seem like a complete distraction from the main enemy. It was as if Blade were trying to get the humans to come against the wolves again so he could be the one who looked like the good guy. Or maybe it was even as simple as the fact that if the humans took out the Talons, then Blade wouldn't have to. She didn't understand how an insane Alpha worked, but she knew the man had plans.

Plans that apparently included her. She didn't think his scheme had anything to do with the fact that she was Kameron's mate. No one had known that other than she and Kameron. So that meant it had to be her connection to Dawn and Aimee and the Talons as a whole. That meant Cheyenne might be in danger, as well. Thankfully, Kameron had sent a couple of wolves who weren't out in public as shifters to watch over Cheyenne. Their friend wasn't happy about it. Frankly, Cheyenne was pissed off that all of this was happening at all, but she was allowing the two wolves to take care of her protection—at least for the short-term. Everyone was trying to do their best to keep the innocent safe, but things were getting so complicated that Dhani had no idea how she'd ended up at this place.

At least the idea of Cheyenne standing in her vet office with two werewolves and countless puppies and kittens that might be afraid of the big, bad wolves, soothed her some. Cheyenne would be safe. Once Dhani completed this farce of a ceremony; hopefully, all of her friends would be safe.

How had things ended up like this? One day, she was flirting with Kameron; the next, they were fighting. One day, they were kissing; the next, they were pushing each other away for the good of their people. At least the good of *his* people. Now, they would be her people too, and she had no idea what she was going to do about that. She'd been right before in thinking that she needed to consider who she was now before she made any changes. But she hadn't had time for that.

The idea that her humanity could be over soon wasn't lost on her. It was the echoing ebb in her brain that worried her. She loved her friends, loved shifters too for that matter, but she hadn't thought she would ever be one. And there were no true human members of the Pack. Eventually, they all became shifters. Or they left. Because watching your friends never age while you grew in your years couldn't be easy.

But now she might not have that problem.

Except for Cheyenne.

And if she kept thinking about her humanity or the lack thereof; if she kept thinking about the war, and her friends, she wouldn't think about the fact that she was about to create a mating bond with a man she didn't love. A man who didn't love her. A man who didn't *want* to love her. To say that things were messy and complicated was an understatement.

How could this be her life? She had known she was delving deeper and deeper into a world that wasn't the one she'd grown up in, but she had thought she was finally getting a handle on it. And then she kissed Kameron. And touched him. And then they had both pulled away. There'd be no pulling away anymore. She didn't know exactly what happened during a mating bond, but she knew it was a stronger connection than even the pull she felt at this point. They would literally be connecting their souls. Forever. And because wolves were so long-lived, forever was a long time. It wasn't just until the end of their days because there were a lot of them.

And the thing was, if she didn't end up becoming a wolf and she aged normally and died a natural death, she would be forcing Kam into a pain that she couldn't comprehend. She had heard horror stories of what happened when one of a mated pair died. Mitchell had gone through it. So had a few others that she had met only in passing. Somehow, a few of them had found other mates, but it had taken decades. Before that, they had walked as hollow representations of themselves, their souls jagged and parts ripped out by the death of another. And though she did not know if she and Kam would ever have the type of mating that perhaps they each deserved, she couldn't force him into that type of agony. She couldn't force him to watch her die like she would never want to watch him do.

Her life would once again be forever altered because of the decisions of others, and because it was the fate that had been laid before them on a path that seemed so daunting, she didn't know if she could follow it the way she should. But it was all out of her hands now. And soon, she'd be mated to a man that she would have to get to know.

Because she wasn't going to fail. Dhani did not fail. Sure, she'd gotten fired from her job, but she had found another one right away. Yes, she couldn't stop the dreams that never seemed to go away, but she lived through them, and she tried to keep them from ruling her life. She would find a way to make this work, too, even if it took part of her to do so.

But for now, she was standing in a shack in the middle of the forest, alone, waiting for her friends to come and say that it was time for the mating ceremony that she hadn't been expecting. There would be no rose petals, no music. There would be no sweet sense of purpose or a new, overwhelming sense of love that brought her to the edge of the abyss.

Instead, she would make promises that she knew she had to keep. She just hoped Kameron would do the same. Because she was making a new life. She was making a choice...but without love. All because she was friends with people that some thought she shouldn't be. All because her parents had betrayed her, or perhaps they'd betrayed themselves because of an outside force. Regardless, while she knew this whole thing was a *big* thing, much bigger than just her feelings, she also had to find a personal reason to make the promises she was about to make.

So, yes, she stood in a shack, wearing a white dress so she looked as if she were having a real wedding; that way, she could appease the humans who didn't understand. Of course, she didn't understand either, but she was finding her way. Dawn and Aimee had just stepped out for a bit so she could have a few moments to herself, but she could hear the others outside. The soldiers were on patrol around them, and Kameron's family was near, though the children were behind the wards, safety ensconced away.

There would be no crowd, no cameras except for a single one. A lone reporter that they trusted who had nothing to do with the man named Jack. This person got the exclusive, and soon, the world would know. They still had to keep the den safe. They were on high alert in case this truly was a distraction, and Blade was going to come at them. But in the end, she had to dig deep and remember that this day was supposed to be special. It was supposed to be about Kameron and her. But it wasn't. There was no way it could be.

There was a knock on the door, and Dawn stuck her head in, a soft smile on her face. The smile didn't reach her eyes, but Dhani was glad that her friend at least tried.

"Are you ready? Take all the time you need. This day is for you."

Dhani shot Dawn a look. "No, it's not. But that's okay. I'm the one who helped get us into this mess, and I'll be the one that helps get us out."

Dawn and Aimee both walked into the shack that was supposed to be the bridal room or whatever. Aimee must've been standing behind Dawn when the other woman stuck her head through the crack in the door.

"No, this day is also about you," Aimee put in.

Dawn pressed her lips together before speaking. "We can stop this right now. We can find another way. You're about to tie your life, your *soul* to another person. If you're both mates, truly, then when the time is right, you'll have your own experience. One where it's not about threats and politics and everything bad in the world. I'm just so afraid that when you look back on this time, everything's going to be tainted, and you're not going to get the day you truly deserve."

Dhani gave Dawn smile, shaking her head. "Each of us has found our path a little bumpy along the way. None of this is normal, but I don't think *normal* is normal anymore. And I'm sorry that I didn't tell you that I was a potential mate for Kameron, but I needed it to be for myself for a little bit. And in the end, I'm glad that I had at least that part to myself because there's nothing private about what's about to happen."

"I know. But if you're feeling the pull, that means there's something magical about you, too." Aimee sighed. "But then again, I guess we already knew that with how you reacted to the wards. And while I'm sorry that things are turning out the way they are, I'm glad that you'll be one of us. I wasn't ready to move on in this new world without my best friends."

None of them mentioned Cheyenne. That wasn't something they could get into today, not with what was about to happen.

"I guess we should just get this over with. That's not the thing I thought I'd say on my wedding day, but this isn't really a wedding day. And it's not really a mating ceremony. It's something for TV to help cool down the waters. Then, we'll figure out what's going on with the Aspens. But it's okay. Really. Kameron and I are...okay. At least I know we will be. There were reasons we kept things to ourselves and reasons we didn't automatically jump into mating. And those reasons might still be there, but there's no going back. We'll figure it out."

Before her friends could question her, she smoothed out the soft white of her dress front and moved towards the door. Dawn and Aimee immediately backed out of the shack, letting Dhani make her way to Kameron.

Her breath caught in her throat, and she did her best not to think about anything but him. This could be just about them, even if it were just in her mind. Because she knew if she thought about anything else, if she let any of the worries she had left back in the shack come with her, she would forever regret this day. She had to think of the future, had to think about who she would be as a mate instead of a woman on the outside looking in. She couldn't think about what Kameron might regret, she couldn't think about any of that pain.

She stood in front of him, and he took her hand. Gideon was saying something, and she knew the camera was rolling, but she only had eyes for Kameron. He wore a suit without a tie, looking cleaner and more striking than ever before. His strong jaw wasn't tensed, not like usual. Instead, he looked right back at her, a promise in his gaze that she hoped she wasn't imagining.

Because if all of this were for nothing, if she were left alone and aching, she didn't know if she could bear it. She was strong, so damn strong, yet the idea that she could be wrong almost cut her off at the knees. Gideon said other things, and she answered, having been coached in what to say for a mating ceremony that wasn't under the full moon. She knew the world was watching, knew they needed her to be sincere, and yet she could only be herself. There was nothing more sincere than that. Kameron reached down and tucked a piece of hair behind her ear, and she smiled softly. Others spoke, using words that weren't those of a traditional ceremony, but words she knew were truth nonetheless.

And when Kam lowered his head to brush his lips along hers, she sank into him, not for the cameras, not for the others, but for her. For him.

The world had seen her make her promises, and later would see her statement that she'd written out before this. But that was all they would get from her. That was all she would lay bare. She couldn't hear what the others were saying, couldn't hear anything except for her own beating heart in her ears. Couldn't feel anything except for Kameron's breath on her cheek.

She wasn't mated, not yet, but that would come soon. That he had made promises, and so had she, had to mean something.

It had to.

CHAPTER THIRTEEN

D hani found herself in Kameron's cabin, her hands shaking like a virgin bride. The idea made her laugh, and Kameron gave her a look.

"I'm glad that you're laughing because this is awkward as hell. And I hate that it's awkward because it shouldn't be, dammit."

He ran his hand through his hair, and she smiled up at him. "I'm laughing because I was just thinking of myself as a shaking virgin bride and I'm totally not. Not really a bride, and sadly, not a virgin. Not that it's sad that I'm not a virgin, but I'm just letting you know. Because I think we need to talk about our sexual history. Or maybe that's something we should have talked about before this. You know, because you're like a century older than me, and I assume you're not a virgin wolf. If you are, I can totally lead you through this and make sure you're comfortable...and I should just shut up now because I'm rambling and I think I'm going to throw up."

With that, Kameron blinked before he threw his head back and laughed. "Thank you for that. No, I'm not a virgin. The idea that you wanted to make sure that I'm comfortable and cared for through this whole thing, though, it's nice. Sweet? I don't know, but I think it makes me like you even more. And yes, the few times we spoke before this, your friends mentioned an ex-boyfriend or two, and at your age, I assumed you weren't a virgin. And now I'm going to stop talking about former lovers because my wolf is ready to tear through my skin and start growling before I go find those guys and rip out their throats. Not really the best thing to be thinking about on the night of our mating ceremony."

"Are you jealous?" She'd never really had a man get jealous when it came to her before. She kind of liked it.

"Of course, I'm jealous. Others had their hands on you. And despite the fact that we've both decided to take things slow and try to figure out exactly what we wanted before this, you're still my mate. So, we're not going to talk about previous men. I will not talk about previous women. By the way, the list isn't that long, even with as many years as I have under my belt—thanks for making me feel old, by the way—because I'm an asshole and I don't like people. But I guess you already figured that out."

"The asshole part, or the not liking people part? I kind of figured out both. But deal, we will not talk about that part of our pasts, but I want to know everything else. I'm not saying right now, but we're stuck in this together. And I didn't mean the word *stuck*. I'm just...I think I'm nervous. I didn't think I'd be this nervous. But I am."

Kameron came up to her and cupped her face. She immediately calmed even as her heart raced. How this man did that to her every time, she didn't know.

"I think I'm a little nervous, too. Before we take the next step, though, I know that you're not a hundred percent okay with what happened today. I'm not either. A mating ceremony should be private. And I'm a very private person. And I know we didn't perform a true mating ceremony today, but later, when the time is right, maybe just you and I can stand under the moonlight and make this happen again. Gideon can be there or not, he's already blessed us. But for some reason, I'm more a man of tradition than I thought. And I don't like the idea that something so tainted is the one ceremony we think of."

Tears filled her eyes, the sincerity in the depth of his emotions surprising her even though they shouldn't. There was a reason she was attracted to this man, and it wasn't just his sexy looks or the pull between them. He was so much more than the icy Enforcer.

"I think I would like that. But this next part, I don't know what I'm doing. So maybe I am that blushing virgin."

"The mechanics of mating? We can talk about that."

"I know about marking. I know about how when you mark my shoulder with your fangs it connects your wolf to me. And when I become a wolf, I'll have to mark you, too." She wasn't going to comment on the latter part again because she wasn't ready." I get that part. I also get that we're not going to use a condom because wolves can't get diseases, and you can't give them to me, and in order for our human souls to connect, we need that part of sex. I know that you're not going to get me pregnant tonight. Or you shouldn't. And I'm on birth control anyway so I should be okay. I get the mechanics. I just don't know what's going to happen once it's over. And I think I'm nervous because I really want to kiss you, but we haven't really gone past that."

He let out a breath, resting his forehead on hers. "What if we just let this be us? What if I kiss you now? What if you kiss me back? And what if I taste you? What if we let the temptation that we've both been ignoring come to the surface? I want to see you, want to touch you. I want to mark you as mine. I've always wanted to, even if we had our reasons to stay away. So let me kiss you, and we can just be us. We can worry about the other things later. Because I need to kiss you."

And because he said the exact right thing, she went up on her toes and kissed him, not wanting to wait any longer. Kameron growled against her lips, the soft bristles of his beard rubbing along her cheek as he nipped down her jaw.

"Just us. Tonight. It's just about us." She breathed the words, practically panting at just being near him. He made her want, made her ache, and if they could have just this moment, then maybe they could have others, too.

His hands roamed her body, going down to cup her ass as he rocked into her, his long, thick, hard erection pressing into her belly. She shivered at the contact, the anticipation of when he'd finally fill her breathtaking.

"Fast or slow?" he asked, a caress of breath against her lips.

She reached between them, grazing the back of her knuckles over the length of his cock. "How about both?"

He licked her lips before gently biting down. "I like the way your mind works."

"Then how about you strip off your shirt because I've really liked the way you've been walking around without one most of the time. It's played in my fantasies even if I've pretended it hasn't."

He grinned at her, the action shocking her because he didn't smile often, and it made his face look so different. He was sexy no matter what he did, but he looked...lighter when he smiled. As if he didn't have the weight of the Pack and maybe even the world on his shoulders.

When he stepped back and slowly undid each button on his shirt before letting the fabric fall to the floor, she sucked in a breath at the sight of him.

He was all hard muscle, lean and tight. She wanted to lick every inch of him, and the realization that he was her *mate* and she *could* hadn't sunk in yet.

"You know, I've had a few fantasies about you walking around without your shirt, as well, but I've never had first-hand experience seeing that."

She raised a brow, not blushing, but totally turned on. This was about them, she reminded herself, no one else, and they could have fun if they wanted to. The real world could wait for them to have one evening together.

"I'm wearing a dress, so you might have to help me. Oh,

and by the way, with the lines on this, I'm not wearing a bra *or* panties. The dress came with a built-in bra, but I'm bare otherwise." And she wasn't the most endowed woman when it came to her breasts, so she could just barely get away with it in this dress.

Kameron's eyes went gold, and she knew that meant the wolf was at the surface. She'd never made love with a man who was also a shifter before—at least to her knowledge—and she knew this would be different.

Perhaps harder.

Perhaps longer.

Perhaps...*more.*

She couldn't freaking wait.

He prowled around to her back, and her breath caught. Then he slowly unzipped her, his warm breath on the back of her neck as he bent forward. The coolness of the room swept up her bare back, and she swallowed hard at the dueling sensations.

When he slid his fingertips under the cap sleeves of her dress and pulled them down, she shivered in his hold. He slowly traced his fingers down her spine as the dress fell to the floor at her feet. The idea that she was completely naked before him while he wore only his suit pants made her want to go down on her knees to take off his pants...and then suck him down her throat because she wanted her mouth on him, just as she wanted his mouth on her.

Their sexual chemistry had never been a problem, and the burning desire within her right then was a vivid reminder.

"You're so fucking beautiful." He slid his fingers over the globes of her butt before tracing the crease of her ass with a single finger. She almost bent over right there for him but knew she wanted to see him naked first. She had priorities, after all.

"I want to see you," she whispered, licking her suddenly dry lips.

He walked around her, kissed her hard on the lips, then went to his knees in front of her. "Soon."

Then he pressed his lips to her pussy, and she gripped his shoulders, her knees going weak. She gasped as he spread her with his fingers, licking and sucking at her until she had to put her weight on him or she'd fall. He explored her pussy, tasting her as if he were devouring a feast, making humming noises and growling as he continued to eat her out with abandon. And when he bit down on her clit, she came right there, unabashed and free.

"Kameron. I need you. Now."

He rose to his feet, holding her close, his lips wet with her orgasm before he kissed her. She could taste herself on him, and she knew she'd gotten even wetter. His dick pressed against her through his pants, and it was all she could do not to wrap her legs around him and ride him like a pony. Her hands roamed his bare back, and his went to her breasts, cupping and pinching and turning her on even more.

He licked and sucked over the wisp of flame scar below her breast, giving her a look that said he had questions, but she had no answers for him. She never had. But just the gentle act of him kissing and sucking on that mark almost made her come again.

And then they were on the hardwood floor, his pants next to them as they explored each other's bodies. He had his hand between her legs, fucking her with his fingers as she arched into him. Her hand was on his dick, her fingers barely able to touch he was so thick, and she knew he would fill her up to the point where she would probably have trouble walking later. And she didn't care.

When he hovered over her, his cock at her entrance, she spread her legs for him and pulled his head down for a kiss. There was nothing to say, no breathing, no words needed. Just him stretching her as he slowly filled her, inch by inch. She arched into him, her nipples pressing into the hair of his chest. The sensation almost sent her over the edge; his body was so perfect for hers. It was as if every single step she'd ever taken had been for this moment. As if every choice she made had led to this path. She'd never been one to believe in fate, rather she had always been one to know that she might have to run from it.

When Kameron met her eyes, she slowly ran the back of her hand along his jaw, across his cheek, and she knew that this moment had changed everything. Because they weren't just doing this for the good of the Pack. Some part of each of them was doing this for the other—and for themselves.

There were no words, there didn't need to be. They spoke with their bodies, moving as one as they took it slow. They might've joked about taking it fast, but she didn't want this moment to end. Because once it did, everything would change, and she would have to think about what came next.

His fangs elongated, and she instinctively turned her head to the side, baring her neck. He slowly licked the part of her neck where it met her shoulder before biting down. His teeth slid into her skin, but it didn't hurt. Instead, a rush of pleasure slammed into her, making her come around his cock. He groaned against her flesh, and they both continued moving their hips, slowly making love as they took each new step into what would be their future.

And when he came inside her, she met his gaze, the gold around his irises so bright she knew she would never see anything like it again.

Then something snapped inside her, a connection she'd never thought possible. The ice and heat of his soul wrapped around hers, the tumultuous chasm of pride and pain sliding deep into her pores. He was hers, and she was his. She knew him, knew him more than she ever thought possible.

And that scared her.

Because her soul knew his.

And now the woman needed to know the man.

The male above her was her mate. Now and forever. There would be no going back. There'd no longer be a time when she thought she could just remain human with just one foot in the world of the supernatural. Kameron was hers. For better or worse. And because of that thought, she turned her head away and kissed his neck. She couldn't see the regret in his eyes, didn't want to know if he felt he had been forced into this. She didn't want to know that she wasn't good enough.

Because she hadn't been good enough before this.

And she wasn't sure she could handle it if it happened again.

Not with him.

Not with Kameron.

CHAPTER FOURTEEN

Somehow, they made it back to his bedroom in the wee hours of the morning, and Kameron watched as Dhani slept beside him. He hadn't meant to take her so roughly against the hardwood floor of his cabin, but he liked that they hadn't gone traditional. Because nothing about them was traditional.

He could feel her within him and could barely keep up with his own breathing. She deserved far more than a man who wasn't sure he could give her anything. But he would try. He hoped he could. Because he had to keep her safe. And the more he felt her within him, the more he touched her, the more he knew that keeping her safe meant possibly keeping her safe from him. Because he wasn't a nice man. He'd tried to be at one point. But when he tried to melt the ice, others died around him. And he couldn't let that happen again. But he would try to do what was right for her.

His heart beat rapidly, and he attempted to tamp down his wolf, but he knew he needed air. He needed to feel the moon on his skin, even if it was just a sliver at this point. There were still a few more hours of moonlight before the sun rose. He would use those. Dhani would be safe in his home, wrapped in sheets that smelled of them both, in a bed that had cradled them both.

She was his mate—body and soul. And he hadn't expected her.

He hadn't expected any of this.

He gently laid a kiss on her brow, holding back a smile at the way she scrunched up her nose. He'd never watched her sleep before. He'd never been in the same bed with her before. Things were moving fast, even for how shifters worked.

But they would make do. They would find their way. Because Dhani was one of the strongest women he'd ever met in his life, and he wasn't going to take that—or her—for granted. Even if it hurt in the end.

As carefully as he could, he slid out of bed and tucked her in again once he was out. He didn't want her to get cold. This whole protective thing had always been a part of him, but he hadn't known it would extend to the way he treated his mate. Perhaps he had hoped it would, but he hadn't known. He couldn't help but think about what would happen if she got hurt because of him. What if she died because of him?

He fought to catch his breath as he staggered out of the house, completely naked, knowing no one would notice since it was so late and he was just going to shift soon anyway. He needed to run as a wolf, needed to feel the wind in his fur as he raced through the forest until his body and mind were one with the world around him. He knew some part of him was going to hate himself for leaving his mate in their bed the night of their mating ceremony, but he couldn't stay and panic.

He fell to his knees as soon as he got a few feet from the house, his hands digging into the soil. His body hurt, not from the exertion of the night before but from holding so much back. He was a shifter, far stronger than the woman who was still in his bed. He could break her without even trying, and he wasn't only talking about her soul. She was so weak as a human, but he knew that she valued her humanity. As she damn well should. He valued who he was, so why shouldn't she? Yet she was going to lose that part of herself when the time came, and he might hate himself for that.

He let out a shaky breath, his body staggering under the weight and depth of the emotions. She was life itself. Deep. A breath of hope, energy, and strength. And he had spent his century on earth burying everything deep inside him that could possibly resemble what she was. Because he couldn't be who he needed to be for his people if he allowed that energy into him. And now he was mated to the one woman who could break him.

Perhaps it was time for him to be broken.

Before he could think too hard on those thoughts, his cousin slid out from the trees wearing an old pair of sweats and no shirt. Kameron hadn't seen Max like this since before the attack. He did his best not to look at the scars or the way Max's arm had healed. The idea that his cousin was able to show any part of himself was a step that Kameron didn't want to hinder.

"Let's go for a run."

Kameron nodded, and with that, Max stripped, went to his knees, and both of them started the shift. Kameron tugged on the cord that connected him to his wolf, bringing his wolf to the forefront. Shifting wasn't easy. In fact, it was painful and long. He wished it were like in the old movies where everything was sparks of light and happiness, but the reality was nothing like that. Instead, his bones broke and reformed. Tendons snapped before tying themselves back together in new ways. His face elongated into the wolf's muzzle, and soon, he found himself standing on four legs, fur covering his body as a wolf rather than a man.

Max took just a bit longer since he wasn't as dominant, and perhaps even longer than he had before the incident. But now, his cousin stood on three legs, his head raised high. And with one final nod, the two of them took off and ran as wolves, the moon pulling them.

Kameron let the man go back, and the wolf come forward, going on instinct alone. He couldn't think too hard when he was in this form, couldn't let the man take over, or he would trip and stumble. Just like in his human form. He couldn't let the wolf take over, or he would trip and stumble in different ways. Only now if he were to do so, he might injure Dhani, as well.

And that wasn't something he would allow himself to do.

He and Max ran for an hour before his cousin headed back to his own place and Kameron loped towards his cabin. He didn't know if Dhani would be up, but he hoped that she wouldn't wake alone. However, as soon as he caught sight of her sitting on the porch with a cup of coffee in her hands, he knew she must've woken up soon after he had left.

He almost started to shift back but realized that she hadn't seen him in this form before. Since he was both the man and the wolf, he wanted her to know both. He wasn't sure if he was making the right decisions when it came to her, but he didn't want to purposely make the wrong ones either.

He walked right up to her on the porch and sat next to her chair. She didn't look hesitant at all, and he knew that she knew who he was. After all, he could feel the bond between them pulsate as it tried to settle into what would be their eventual true mating bond.

Right now, it was erratic. Eventually, they might learn if there were any more connections that came with it. Some mates could read each other's thoughts. Others could send pulses of different emotions down the bond. And even more could sense exactly where the other was at any given time. He knew there were other powers that went along with some of the mating bonds, but it depended on the people involved. He had an inkling that his bond with Dhani wouldn't settle completely until she was a shifter, and both of their wolves could find each other.

"I don't think I've ever seen you as a wolf. Or maybe I have, but only in the distance. You're quite pretty. But how do you not have hair all over your place?"

He rolled his eyes, and she laughed. He was not a dog, but it wasn't as if he could tell her that. She set down her coffee cup on the side table and loosened the blanket around her shoulders. She had put on his button-up shirt from the day before and wore no panties or pants. He held back a growl because not only did he not want her to be cold, he sure as hell didn't want anyone to see her like this. He might've wanted to keep her safe before they mated, but it was nothing like his instincts now. And he'd be damned if he let anybody near her when she was just wearing his shirt. She was his, and the world would just have to get used to that.

"Can I pet you? I mean, I know you're not a dog. But I've always wanted to feel what your fur is like. Is that weird?"

In answer, he slid his head under her outstretched hand and leaned into her. Her smile was wide as she slowly slid her fingers through his fur. If he were a cat, he would've been purring at that point. As it was, he did his best not to shake his leg like a dog would at the feel of her hand on his body.

He knew this was hard for her. Knew that it was a step both of them had wanted to wait to take; one they might not have taken at all if the time weren't right. But now that they were together, he would do everything in his power to make sure she understood that she was treasured, even if their mating wasn't like everyone else's.

He knew the ramifications of what they had done would come soon. But for now, he would lean into his mate and let her pet him. As she smiled when he slowly used his teeth to tighten the blanket around her, he thought maybe they could make this work.

Maybe he could have a mate *and* keep her safe.

Maybe he hadn't doomed her to a fate neither of them was ready for.

MAX

Max hid behind the trees, watching the newly mated couple as Kameron let Dhani pet him as if she were the only one in his world. In all his life, Max had never thought to see his cousin react like that. He'd always hoped, of course. Had always thought that maybe, just maybe there would be a woman that could make Kameron let down his shields, but he hadn't expected it to be Dhani.

Maybe that was why it worked.

But Max didn't know much of anything anymore it seemed.

Didn't even know who he was.

Because he didn't like the idea that he wasn't the nice one anymore. He didn't like how he was treating those who loved him. But he didn't know how to stop being this new Max. He didn't know how to stop being so angry all the time. He didn't know how to stop hurting.

He didn't know anything.

And now he was the only Brentwood left without a mate. Every other sibling and cousin had found theirs, even if they had taken the hard road to get there. But now they would all find their happiness. He knew Kameron and Dhani had a long path to follow to find that happily ever after, but they would get there. He had to believe it.

Because he didn't really believe in anything anymore. At least not *much* of anything.

He was the only one left. The only one without someone to share his soul with. And maybe that was a good thing. Because he was broken. Something had been taken from him, and not just a limb. He knew he wasn't a shell of a man because of that. It went deeper than that…deeper than he knew how to comprehend. Because he was whole, yet not. And it had nothing to do with his physical body.

Once he had thought he might find his mate and show her the world that he loved and thrived in. That wasn't the case anymore. Some part of him still thought there might be a woman that could be his. But even though the mating bonds had been fixed, he was so numb, he couldn't really feel anything anymore. But maybe that was for the best.

Because he wasn't the same man he'd once been.

Until he could discover the man he was now, he wouldn't be the type of man a mate needed.

He wouldn't be the wolf they needed.

He wouldn't be Max. Whoever that was.

CHAPTER FIFTEEN

This time, the dream pulled her in so quickly, so violently, that Dhani couldn't catch her breath. Instead, she fought, trying to claw her way back out of the dream. Because she knew nothing good could come of it, nothing that would keep her safe and whole anyway. Something was coming, she'd always known that, but as the dream wrapped its spindly fingers around her waist, pulling her down into the abyss, she knew there would be no waking up this time until the dream wanted her to.

So she fell.

The older woman was back again, this time staring at her. Dhani was part of the dream, rather than an observer, though. There was a baby crying in the distance, but she couldn't see where it was coming from. There was another woman crying, a man trying to soothe her, but Dhani didn't know where they were. All she could do was look at the older woman who stared at her. Then the woman spoke.

"Stand up. You stood up. Open up. You've opened up. But you must give up. Not now, but soon. Because, remember, sacrifice begets sacrifice. You are strong. Remember that, child. You are *strong*."

Then Dhani screamed and woke up.

Only, unlike every other time, she wasn't alone.

"Dhani? What's wrong? Are you hurt?" Kameron hovered above her, his gaze intense as he searched her face before running his fingers down her cheek.

She sucked in a breath, her body coated in a thin sheen of sweat as she fought to slow her heart rate. "I'm okay."

Kameron glared, his wolf in his eyes. His face lowered to hers, his breath warm on her cheek. "You're lying. I get that you're scared, but you're lying. You don't get to lie to me. We don't get to lie to each other. Not anymore. We're mates, remember? Talk to me. What just happened?"

They were mates. She still couldn't quite comprehend that. The idea that she could still feel his soul wrapped around hers was something she knew would take eons to fully understand.

"Dhani." His voice was low, not a growl but the kind of need she yearned for.

She shook her head and looked up into Kameron's eyes. He was still hovering over her, their legs tangled as they lay naked in his bed. Or maybe *their* bed.

Strange how things had changed so quickly.

"It was just a nightmare. I get them sometimes. I'm

sorry." Sorry for waking him up, that was. She'd never lay in bed with a man before when she was thrown into a dream like that. Maybe she hadn't been able to trust anyone enough to allow herself to fall into her dreams like that.

Or maybe whatever had led her to have the dreams in the first place knew that Kameron should be a part of it.

And there went that sense of knowing again.

Kameron shook his head and sat up. The sheet pooled around his waist, and her gaze followed his happy trail down to the dark shadow of his lap. She licked her lips but forced her eyes to his as she sat up, as well. She was still a little shaky from her dream and being near him, but she wanted to be on the same level with him as she spoke. She needed to be.

"Don't be sorry. You didn't do anything wrong except lie to me. But, really, I probably would have lied too. Since, like you, I don't like others knowing what I'm feeling or thinking." He ran a hand down his jaw, his beard growing in since he hadn't shaved the day before. She'd liked the way it had felt against her skin, liked the way she was learning more about him with each passing moment. Things were moving far too fast for them, but she was soaking it all in as quickly as she could.

"If I have to tell you everything, does that mean you have to do the same for me?"

His jaw clenched, but he gave her a tight nod. His hand fisted on the sheet beside them and she followed his lean, muscled arm up to his face again. "I'll try."

That was something at least. And if they were going to

sleep in the same bed every night, then he needed to know what he was in for when it came to her dreams. And when it came to her in general.

She'd never had to explain this part of herself before, and she wasn't sure she could, but she'd try. Because he'd risked everything for her, just as she'd done for him. And though she didn't know every aspect of him, she couldn't hide herself anymore.

"I have nightmares that aren't truly nightmares. Ever since I can remember, I've had dreams where they feel like...*more*. They're not always so serious, but sometimes, it almost feels like a knowing. I've told you about that before, how I can almost feel where I need to be or what decision I need to make. That's the basis of my dreams. I can't explain it, but I know it's important. Before I knew about shifters and witches and that magic was real, I thought I was crazy. Now, I'm not so sure. But I had a dream tonight, one that scared me."

She told him the words the old woman had spoken, the words Dhani knew were important. She still couldn't wrap her head around them. All she knew was that, somehow, she'd gone through part of what the woman needed her to do, but the hardest steps were yet to come.

She'd been told she was strong. But was she truly strong enough to face what came next?

He sat there a moment, his gaze intense as he listened. "I knew things were different. You'd mentioned it before, but if you want, we can look into it more when you're ready.

Things aren't the same as when you were living in the human world."

That reminded her, "Do you think it will change when I'm a wolf?"

He frowned. "I don't know. Things aren't the same for every human that changes into a wolf. And I don't know what happens when you're changed into a cat." He paused. "I'm thinking you'll go wolf since it requires a dominant or Alpha to change you, and without Audrey, we don't have a cat shifter to start the change. As for these visions of yours, I know Avery is a foreseer, and her visions only became more manageable and clearer once she became a wolf. I don't know why you have these…dreams, though. They sound almost like prophecies, yet they're…different. I don't know what to tell you other than that you're Pack now, so no matter what happens, you won't be alone when everything changes after you shift."

He paused while she tried to come to terms with his words, then he cupped her cheek.

"What?" she asked.

"We never talked about it, but you know what's coming soon. Becoming a shifter isn't easy. It's not for everyone, and it can easily go wrong. The Pack bonds and mating bonds should help, but it's still going to be traumatic. I wish there was another way. Witches can stay as they are because their magic becomes entwined with the mating bond, but that isn't the case for humans. We've searched for a way for those who mate into the Pack to remain their human selves, but there isn't one. For you to remain healthy and stay part of the Pack as you grow older and into the bond, you *will* have to become a shifter. That means Gideon will have to bring you to near death, then bite and tear into you until we're sure the shift will take. Pain meds and any other drugs only hinder the change."

Her hands shook, but she nodded. He put his hand over hers, calming her. This icy, gruff wolf sure knew how to comfort even if he told himself—and her—that he wasn't any good at it. "I know. I talked with Aimee about it. What Audrey and Walker had to do in order to save her life wasn't pleasant, but she's alive now to talk about it. I knew going in that I'd have to leave my humanity behind. I *knew* it, though it doesn't make it any easier. I'm not ready, but I don't know if I'll ever be ready."

Kameron leaned forward and cupped her cheek. "We have time. Let's get used to who we are now with this new bond first, then we'll take the next step. Not to mention, we still don't know what the ramifications are from our very public debut in the human world."

She winced. "I keep trying to suppress the memories of what my parents did. It's not working."

Kameron growled. "Blade. It was *Blade*. It's always been Blade."

She narrowed her eyes. "If I didn't know otherwise, I'd say you have an obsession with the man." She didn't like the idea that Kam was putting the worries and safety of his Pack on his shoulders as he was. Then again, he was the Enforcer. Perhaps that's how they survived.

"He needs to be ended. If it's by my claw, all the better."

"Kameron."

"Don't start. My family and Pack, my *mate,* are all in danger because of that man. I'll stop at nothing to make sure he never has the chance to cause more harm."

Dhani let out a breath. "Then I'll help, too."

"You're a teacher. Your job is to keep our young safe."

The idea that she actually had a place in the Pack was something that warmed her, but she wasn't done yet. "Yes, but as your mate, it's my job to keep *you* safe and sound. Emphasis on the latter since you're the big, bad wolf and I'm the human here."

He lowered his head and kissed her softly. "We'll figure this out. All of it." His chest rumbled as the sheet fell from her grasp and landed at her waist, leaving her breasts bare to him. "But first…"

She snorted, then moaned as he licked his way down her neck. It seemed they were going to banish the serious thoughts of the morning in the best way possible. And now that he was *hers* in at least some of the ways she was just learning, she could indulge.

Finally.

He explored her mouth as she slid her hands up and down his back, her nails digging in as he moved down slightly to suck on her neck. Her breaths started coming in short pants as he rocked against her. They were both already naked, his rock-hard cock pressing against her wet heat. If she angled her hips just right, he'd slide right in. And since she already knew she was soaked, he'd glide in to the hilt easily, and she'd probably come immediately.

But since Kameron was who he was, he put a hand on her hip, stalling her.

"Not yet. I'm going to taste you. Touch you. Feel you. Then, after you've come a few times, I'll fuck you hard into the mattress."

Her eyes rolled back as he played with her nipple after he moved his hand from her hip. He rested on his other arm so he didn't put weight on her and the action moved his cock away from her heat. She would have pouted, but his hands on her felt far too good for her to complain right then.

Instead, she let her legs spread, and her hands continue to roam over his body. His skin was so smooth, yet it had a roughness to it that told her his body had healed over and over from battles. He didn't have as many scars as she might have thought because he healed so quickly, but Kameron had a warrior's body, and she craved more of it.

"I love your nipples. They're just the right size for my mouth. It's like you were made for me."

"Funny that," she said on a pant. "Your cock is just the right size for me."

He looked up and grinned, and she knew she could fall for that expression. He rarely smiled, but when he did, it made her heart hurt in the best possible way. This man, this wolf, was *hers*, and she was enjoying getting to know all parts of him—more than she thought she would. Maybe the moon goddess knew exactly what she was doing when she put the two of them together.

Kameron's mouth trailed down her belly and then

moved between her legs. The blanket had long since fallen to the floor, and she went up on her elbows so she could watch him taste her. The strong muscles of his butt flexed as he moved, his back wide and rippling with strength. This was *her* man, and damn he had a talented tongue.

When he started to tease her entrance with his fingers then slowly slid them into her, curling the digits and finding that special spot inside, she arched her back, her head falling back so her hair splayed across the sheet below them both. She called out his name as she came, but he didn't let up. Instead, he held onto her hips, demanding more. And because she could feel the need, the craving along the bond, she came again.

His eyes were gold when he looked up, his mouth wet from her desire. Then he placed his feet on the floor, grabbed her hips, and flipped her over onto her stomach.

"On your knees," he growled.

Her body seemed to immediately heed his command, and yet she was just fine with that. She went up onto her knees as his hands dug into her hips. Then he slammed into her with one intense thrust, and she knew she would be lost again at any moment.

He pumped in and out of her, his cock stretching her as she moved her hips to meet him thrust for thrust. He was so wide, so long that she knew she'd be sore later, yet she knew it would be an ache she'd savor.

This man knew *exactly* what he was doing to her, and from the grunts and growls behind her, he liked what she was doing to him, as well.

Good.

When he pulled out all the way, she rolled out of the way and turned so she could pull him down. Thankfully, he let her and went to his back on the bed. She quickly straddled him, took his dick in her hand, and slowly slid down his length.

They both let out a groan when she was fully seated, then she gave him a grin. "Ready for me to ride?"

"It's about time I get to play with these pretty breasts." Then he did, and she moved, her body rolling over his as the orgasm came again.

And when she was finally out of breath, out of *everything*, she went to her back, and he rolled with her, finally coming inside her as he growled her name. Then he bit her again, marking her as his, and she knew she'd forever remember this moment. This man. This wolf.

Her man. Her wolf.

Hers.

CHAPTER SIXTEEN

Kameron hated waiting. He had never been patient, even though with his position he had to be more patient than some. He always had to find the right time to either attack or be on the defensive. He had to strategize, collect all the facts, and then present them to his brother and Alpha.

But it didn't make waiting any easier.

Waiting to see how humans would react to Dhani becoming a Pack member, to becoming his mate, was a new form of torture. He was still trying to get used to the fact that she was his. Everywhere he walked around the den, he could feel a slight pulse inside his chest that told him she was near. He didn't know what would happen to them eventually, what would happen to their bond as it evolved, but he knew that this moment was important.

And in order for what they were and everything that

was to come to *remain* important, he needed to know what was going to happen next.

He also knew more than most that there was no telling what would happen next. No foreseers or prophecies like his mate was most likely seeing would help him find the right path.

Kameron knew that things would have to change. He couldn't just hide his mate away inside the den wards and pretend that everything was going to be okay. Because it wouldn't be. The world needed to see that she was free to come and go as she pleased and that she wasn't a chained-up bride or whatever the tabloids were saying. And though he wanted to wrap her in cotton wool and hide away from the world, he knew that wasn't something he could do. Not only would it be wrong, but Dhani would kick his ass.

In the past, when he thought about what his mate could be, *who* she would be, he hadn't pictured Dhani. He'd pictured someone he could protect, someone a little... softer, maybe even a maternal dominant. But that wasn't Dhani. Yes, she took care of the Pack's young, but there was nothing submissive or inherently maternal about her. Those weren't the right words... Because she was amazing with pups, but she was also far more dominant in her human form than any of the others in her position. And he had a feeling that stark contrast would become even more evident, and she would become even fiercer once she became a shifter.

Dhani would never stand by and let him protect her. She was going to face whatever came at her by his side. Had she done that when they made their relationship public? She had thrown herself into ensuring that the people around her were safe by doing something she wasn't ready for. She hadn't thought of herself, only those she loved. Maybe that was exactly the mate he needed.

Except for the fact that he hadn't wanted a mate who would be in danger just by being connected to him. Everything was slipping through his fingers, and he was just trying to catch up.

But even though he didn't feel as if he were quite where he needed to be, he knew what they needed to do next. As if he'd conjured her out of thin air, his mate walked up to him and gave him a strange look.

Was it wrong that he liked that expression? That it turned him on?

The mating bond was truly changing him.

"We don't have to do this, you know. We can just stay inside the den wards. Screw what people think."

"We both know that's not something either of us is willing to do. We're just going to walk outside like I'm on a normal patrol, but this time, you're going to be by my side. We'll still be on Pack territory, just not in the den itself. So there will be no wards to protect us or shield us from any prying eyes. But it means that any curious observers can see that you're free to come and go as you please. And that you're safe."

"Of course, I'm safe. I'm your mate. I think being the mate of the Enforcer and by his side, contrary to what you believe, is a pretty safe place to be."

He held back the growl that wanted to escape his lips and gave her a short nod. His mate was never going to be in a safe place. Because she was a symbol that any enemy could use against them. Any mate of those in the hierarchy would always be a symbol and in danger. But the mate of the one who was supposed to protect the Pack? That was even worse—at least in his experience and that of the other Enforcers he'd met along the way.

"We should get going. Smile a lot, and make it look like you're having fun."

She rolled her eyes. "Oh, yes, a romantic walk with my mate while we're still trying to get to know each other will be so difficult. Excuse me while I plaster a smile on my face and pretend. You do realize that if we actually act like we like each other, it won't be acting. You're stuck with me for a long time, Kam. You better get used to it. And me."

He shook his head. "The thing is, I don't think I'm ever going to get used to you. But I don't know if that's a bad thing."

"That was sweet. And I'm going to take it as a compliment."

"You should. Now, let's go over what we talked about before. You're going to be by my side no matter what. My trackers and soldiers will be around, but we're not going to be able to see them. That's their job. I won't be on actual patrol, but knowing me, I'll still be searching. We don't have you trained with weapons yet, and that's something we need to fix. I'm your protection. Meaning, if something happens, you *will* do exactly as I say. Even if what I say is to run full-tilt back to the den. I'm not saying that anything will happen, but you have to listen to me if it gets bad. Okay?"

"I can do that." She frowned. "But I don't know how I could ever run away if you're in danger."

"You'll just have to learn to do it. Because right now, you're one of the weakest among us. I'm not talking about what's inside because we damn well know that's not the case since I can feel your soul inside me. But if I say run, you run. As it is, I'm going to be distracted, trying to make sure you're safe while protecting myself. I can do that, but I also need to know that you can listen to my orders."

"I don't take orders well. But I'll do my best for you." She paused. "Of course, I haven't really been taking orders in sex yet either, not that you've given me many since you sort of just toss me around however you want me. I kind of like that, though. Maybe we can talk about orders in bed a little bit later, too." The tips of her ears went red, and Kameron had to adjust himself in his jeans even as he growled. Yes, this woman would be the death of him, but he thought he might perhaps like it.

"What did I tell you about getting me hard when I have to be in public?"

"That it is your favorite thing ever and I should continue trying to make you hard? Maybe I should even stroke a bit?"

He leaned down and bit her lip, not too hard, but enough that her eyes widened. "Enough. For now."

And with that, he took her hand and led her through the wards. Even though she was part of the Pack now, her body still shook slightly as she went through the magic. He had a feeling that had to do with that *knowing* she had talked about. They were going to have to delve deeper into that eventually—but one thing at a time.

Thankfully, their walk was boring if comfortable. They talked about what her new lesson plans would be, and how she still wanted to talk to her parents even if it would be hard. She did most of the talking, while he just listened. That was how he usually was, so it wasn't as if this were different than any other person. But it *was* different. This was his mate, and perhaps she deserved more than just his listening. Maybe she deserved more of him. Only he never thought to be in this position, and he still felt as if he were two steps behind.

Maybe that wasn't fair, considering she was the one who'd been thrown into a completely new world. Maybe she was the one who was supposed to be behind, and he should be showing her the way. Only it felt like it was the opposite, and that just showed how strong this woman was. She was *his*. And that was something he would have to get used to.

He held back a sigh and focused on the woman beside him and what their job was for the day. To act normal. To blend in. To just *be*. Out of all the wolves in the Pack—except perhaps Max—he would have been the last choice for this job.

He could sense a few humans around, but most of them were right on the edge of Pack territory, watching. He didn't mind that. That was what this walk was for, after all. It didn't make him feel any less uneasy, however. He still felt as if they were parading themselves around. As if they were in some zoo where all the humans paid to see them in their natural habitat. Maybe they would throw snacks and take photos. Next time, he'd bring balloons.

Of course, as soon as he thought that, a flash went off and he turned at the sound. Someone had indeed taken a photo of the two of them. That person was lucky the whole camera thing was part of the PR aspect or he would rip the asshole's face off.

He paused, maybe his wolf was a little too on edge for this walk to really work.

Then Dhani squeezed his hand, and everything felt a little better. Was this how it was supposed to be between mates? He didn't know; hadn't really thought about it. But now it seemed all he was doing was thinking about it.

They were just reaching the end of the territory when the explosion hit. Kameron threw himself on top of Dhani, ignoring the burn on his side and on his back. The scent of magic and humans surrounded him, but there was something…off about it. He didn't quite understand it, but he knew it would be important later.

For now, he pushed those thoughts out of his head and only focused on the woman beneath him, the female screaming his name. He could scent the wolves around them, taking stock of what had happened. A couple of the humans that had been safely taking photos were also on the ground. Kameron cursed and looked at one of his soldiers before nodding towards the downed humans. He didn't think they had anything to do with what was happening, but he didn't know. His people had to be safe and care for their own, but they also couldn't let innocents die on their watch.

And they didn't know if there was another explosion coming.

It hadn't been a huge one, just about the size of a small pipe bomb, he figured, but it was enough that when he sat up and looked down at his mate, he let out a howl. She had blood running down her face from a small cut on her head from flying debris, and she was rubbing her elbow. It didn't look as if she had any broken bones, but she was going to be bruised for sure. Because she was a human. Fragile.

And his mate.

His.

Someone had dared to hurt her.

"I'm fine, Kameron. You're the one bleeding. Let's take you back and take care of you. Walker can Heal you. Let the others take care of this, and let me take care of you. I'm fine." She repeated the last words when he growled, and then she leaned forward and kissed his chin. "I'll be okay. Let's just make sure everyone else is okay. Let me make sure *you're* okay. Whoever did this will be caught. We have to make sure everyone is safe. And that includes you."

He growled again but stood up. His back ached, and he knew Walker would have to Heal him because he had a feeling that whatever had exploded had left stones and other debris embedded in his skin. It was going to hurt like a bitch, but first, he had to take care of his people and his mate. His territory had been attacked, even if it had been a small siege that had only hurt him—at least from what he saw. And he wasn't going to stand for that. The Talons wouldn't stand for that.

So he helped his mate to her feet, wiped the blood from her face, and held her against him before howling. The other wolves howled with him, their song one of protection and anger.

The others from his Pack would be there soon to make sure that everything was okay and that everyone was safe, even as they closed ranks to protect the den itself.

Someone had dared to hurt his mate. Dared to hurt him. Dared to try and hurt others under his protection.

And he thought the scent was human, but he also scented a touch of magic.

He couldn't be sure.

But he would be.

Soon.

TO HEEL

Blade couldn't help but smile. It had been a long time coming, but finally, things were working out in his favor. There had been blood on the ground and screams in the air, and he'd never heard such a symphony of glory. His Pack was going to rule the world, *he* was going to rule the world —or at least he would rule this area.

Because that was all he needed.

The world needed to see his strength. See what he had done over his lifetime.

And they would know that he was the one the world needed for their salvation.

And though they didn't have the last two human women in their clutches yet, they would. Because one of them had bled, one of them had screamed. It didn't matter that she was mated into the damn Talon Pack now. She was still human; therefore, she was fair game.

Because the Talons thought the humans had attacked them. Because they were stupid. They always fell for what he needed them to believe. They didn't know they had a traitor in their midsts. They didn't know that one of Blade's own lived in their den, lived near their precious humans. They didn't know that Blade was the one with the upper hand.

But they would know soon.

As his red witch finished up the magic that had allowed the traitor to smell like a human, Blade just smiled. He had the best people. He was the best Alpha. And soon, the Talons and the Redwoods would come to realize that. Once the women were sacrificed, the humans would know what terrors lay within their borders, and the Redwoods and the Talons would cease to exist. The humans would be the ones to take them out.

And Blade and the Aspens would prevail.

The humans would bow before him.

And the Redwoods the Talons would be no more.

Finally.

CHAPTER SEVENTEEN

Kameron winced as he settled into bed, but unlike the last time he'd been hurt in the line of duty, he wasn't alone. Dhani sat by his side, her teeth biting into her bottom lip as she watched him move into position. He knew he shouldn't find that sexy since she'd been bleeding in his arms earlier that day, but he couldn't help it when she was around and truly safe and sound. She hadn't been hurt that badly, but it was still enough to set his wolf on edge.

"I'm okay. Really. Walker took care of the major wounds and bruises. I'm just a little sore. And I won't be for long anyway. There are perks to being a shifter."

"You say that, yet you're wincing. You never wince or show weakness."

"Kind of hard to hide it when you're around. You're

literally in my soul, what you see is what you get from me now."

That made her smile, even though there was a deep worry in her eyes. He didn't know where these words were coming from, but it wasn't as if he could hold himself back when it came to her. He'd try around others, but what happened between the two of them was *just* between them, no matter how curious his family might be.

"You say the sweetest things." She fluffed his pillow behind him, and he resisted the urge to roll his eyes. She was worried about him and playing nurse, so he could understand. He'd just never had anyone take care of him before. She gave him a look before asking, "Why are you looking at me like that? Has no one ever fluffed your pillows before? And no, I don't mean that as a euphemism."

She tried to tuck him in, and he reached out, gripping her wrist in a loose hold. "No one's ever fluffed my pillows before."

She let out a breath, staring into his eyes. "I know we said we would never talk about past lovers but do we need to?"

He shook his head. "We don't need to. I never had a mate before you. You're it for me. And you've never been married before this, and though it's not a marriage, we're still us. What I was talking about with the pillows wasn't about an ex-lover, but more of my past."

"Your parents." She was silent for a moment and then bit her lip when he didn't say anything right away. "We don't have to talk about them."

He didn't particularly like this subject, but he knew he needed to at least tell her some things. "I know. And you already know a lot anyway. Kind of hard to miss when you're living in the den with so many Brentwoods who lived through their own Hells with our dad. Mom wasn't bad. Not like him. But she was so beaten down that she *couldn't* protect us. And then she wasn't there anymore. There were a lot of us, more if you include Mitchell and Max, who had their own issues with their father—my uncle. We grew up in Hell and were forced to live in it for a century. Now, we don't anymore."

He didn't know why he was speaking so much since that wasn't his normal thing, but Dhani seemed to bring it out in him. And he wasn't even sure it was just because she was his mate. Not any longer. It was just...her.

He wasn't the touchy-feely type. He was the guy that pushed people away to protect them. And he wasn't sure he would like himself if he changed any more than he already had. But perhaps he wouldn't have to change for others. Only her. Or maybe he was thinking too hard and really just needed to kiss her.

Because he was falling for her. Falling for his mate. He didn't know how it had happened, or when it had started, but it had. He knew part of it was the fact that he was coming to know her strength, her commitment, and the fact that she faced danger no matter the cost. She fit with him, and he wasn't sure what he should think about that. But he also knew that he couldn't hide himself from her. She deserved better, and he was going to provide that. Even if he had no idea what he was doing.

"I hate that you went through that. That any of you guys went through that. And I don't really know what to say other than I know things are different now and yet still dangerous. As someone who teaches children daily, I don't really seem to be good with words right now."

He had never been good with words. He leaned forward and tucked her hair behind her ear. His twinges and aches weren't all that bad, and between his brother's Healing and his own natural shifter ability, he was doing better than Dhani probably figured. Walker was amazing at his role in the Pack, but there were some wounds that just took time. However, Kameron was dominant enough to heal on his own, as well. And that meant he needed to make sure that his mate was okay; needed to make sure that he could hold her.

Because he was still so damn pissed that someone had dared to hurt her. She had a few bruises, but the cut on her forehead hadn't even required stitches. Yet he wanted to tear up those who had dared come for her. He still blamed himself, even though he knew she would get angry that he thought that. But there was no way he could stop. He'd been the one to suggest them walking outside the den so others could see them acting normally, and he had been the one to put her in danger. And she had dealt with the consequences. He might've bled more, but he wasn't human, and he healed faster than she could. After she went through the transformation and was fully a wolf, maybe he would be able to sleep better, but until then, he would just have to deal with the fact that she was far more fragile than he was.

He was still so angry. Always. And there was nothing he could do except try to fix it. Try to keep her safe. Even though he hadn't really been doing a good job of it as of yet.

"You're looking at me like you want to eat me up. But considering you were just thrown down to the ground because of a pipe bomb, shouldn't we be sleeping so you can heal?"

He leaned forward as she spoke the words, and he licked her bottom lip. He loved biting and licking her and hadn't known it would be such a turn on just to be able to have her in his arms. This whole mating thing was new to him, but he was getting used to it. Slowly. He liked to take it slow. And maybe hard. And fast.

Apparently, his dick was ready to go because he was so hard he was about to burst. He shifted slightly, and her gaze went down to his lap, her eyes widening when she caught sight of his erection tenting the sheets.

"I'm almost healed completely. You said you weren't sore. Somehow, we'll take it slow and see what happens." He leaned forward again, and this time, he kissed her lips.

She pulled away slightly, her eyes dark with lust. "I'm not sore. I can take it easy on you if you want."

He growled low, loved the way that her eyes widened when he did so. She was getting used to this whole para-normal thing, and he liked that he was the one helping introduce her to the new things. Yes, she had her friends, but he was part of her life now, too. He didn't know how he'd become so addicted to her so quickly, but here he was. She was in his bed. *Their* bed. And all he wanted to do was have her in his arms.

"We can talk about that whole commanding thing you mentioned if you want."

She bit her lip, and he let out a groan. He loved those lips. "We can try. Maybe. But since you're the one who's hurt, maybe I should do the ordering around." She winked as she said it.

This time, he growled louder, and she laughed. Then she was on her back, and he was on top of her, kissing her as if he couldn't stop; as if he were a man starved for her. Because he was.

But, somehow, she got the upper hand. Suddenly, he was on his back, and she was between his legs, her mouth on his cock. He groaned, his hand sliding through her hair as he fought not to pump his hips. The woman knew exactly how to take care of him, knew exactly what he wanted. And he was learning what she wanted just as much. How he'd thought he could stay away from a mate, how he thought he'd be able to fight her off, he didn't know. But there was one thing he did know, he fucking loved her mouth.

And damn, he was starting to fucking love her, too.

She cupped his balls in her hand and looked up at him, her mouth around his dick, and her eyes looking so fucking sexy he knew he'd blow his load if he weren't careful.

"You want me to come in your mouth or in you?" He should be talking sweetly to his mate, but she wanted orders, she wanted him. That meant she got *him*. All his ice and crass.

She let go of his dick with a wet pop. Fuck. That was way too sexy. As it was, he had to reach down and squeeze the base of his cock so he didn't come on her face or her tits right then. He was a wolf, not an animal.

"You're a shifter. I thought you had all of that stamina I hear about from the girls. Why not both?"

He let out a rough laugh, his dick twitching his in hand. "Then you better get back to blowing me, mate."

She rolled her eyes. "So romantic."

"Please go back to blowing me?" he asked.

"That's polite. Not romantic. But I'll take it." Then she took him in, and he closed his eyes, trying to keep his mind on what he was doing and not the fact he was falling for her. And when she did something special with her tongue, he came. Hard.

He opened his eyes, his body practically shaking, and before he could flip them over so she was on her back, she was on top of him with his back to the headboard.

"You're injured, remember? Let me take care of you."

So he grabbed her hips and helped her slide down his already recovered length. He was always hard when it came to Dhani and they both knew it.

"I can do that." He groaned when she rocked her hips. "I can do that," he repeated; this time, his words coming out in pants.

"This is me taking care of you," she whispered before biting down on his ear. Then she pulled back slightly, and he was able to take one hand, lower his head, and bring her breast up to his mouth. He sucked, licked, and bit down.

He loved his mate's taste. So damn much.

She looked up then, her eyes dark, her mouth parted. He slid his hand from her breast to between them. When he played with her, she sucked in a sharp, shallow breath and came. And because she squeezed his cock, because he could feel her orgasm through the mating bond, he came again.

And then they were lying together on his bed, on *their* bed, and he knew he'd fight to the death for her. He'd fight the world for her.

He'd fight himself for her.

And he had no idea how it had happened.

THE NEXT DAY, Kameron was almost completely healed, yet a small part of him wanted to play injured so his mate could take care of him in their bed. Later that day, they were going to completely move her out of the small cottage and into his house. That way, someone else could have her place, and they could try to figure out how they were going to be mates in this new world. Yes, things were moving quickly, but for a race of immortals, things tended to move fast whenever bonds and magic were involved.

But he hadn't played sick or hurt. Instead, he walked her to the school so she could work and kissed her softly. He ignored the literal wolf whistles and knowing looks. No one had ever seen him like this. But they would just have to get used to it. He would have to get used to it, as well.

Now, he was back to the grind...being the Enforcer. He was back in his office at the soldier barracks rather than the one at his house. When he was working, he liked to be surrounded by his men and women even if he wasn't talking to them. He wanted to be available if they had any questions or if he needed to order them to do something. And though there wasn't as much important paperwork or as many comfortable areas as there were in his home office, he was still able to get some work done before and after his patrols.

Max was by his side, frowning over some notes, but that wasn't anything new. His cousin was constantly frowning over notes as he tried to figure out exactly what needed to be done. In a way, Max was becoming his second in command. They hadn't meant for it to happen, but over the past few years, Kameron had found himself relying on his cousin more and more. Max was smart, determined, and had truly needed a role beyond being a council member after everything that had happened. Kameron had realized that the two quietest Brentwoods of the bunch had come together—still quiet but determined.

But at least he knew Max wasn't alone.

"I hate that we feel like we're missing something. Because I only scented our people and humans out there. But there was that slight trace of magic. And I don't know if I would've scented if I hadn't been looking for it. And then I think I only scented it because I was looking for it. Maybe it wasn't there at all." Kameron growled. "I'm getting a headache."

Max gave him a look before shaking his head. "You sure the headache isn't because you were just thrown to the ground because of a bomb? Because no matter how many times you say it was just a small bomb, it was still a bomb. You sure Dhani's okay?"

"If she wasn't fine, I sure as hell wouldn't be here. I'd probably be outside the den tearing off faces or right by her side. I'm just so fucking angry that someone was able to set the bomb off in the first place. Because that means one of my men or women didn't notice. That means we're still fucking up even though we're still on high-alert. And that means that Blade is still getting the upper hand. Because even though I scented human, I still feel like it has to do with that man."

"Or maybe you're just connecting Blade to everything bad that goes on here. Because you and I both know it's not just some whacko Alpha who's out to get us. Even though the laws changed, not all humans are happy with us. And there's still that human faction that wants us dead—dead or trapped in cages. They might be quiet, but only for the media. They're loud as hell online and in the threatening notes they send."

Max was right. The human contingent that hated anything that wasn't *normal* was still out there. They might not be at all out war with the humans, and the government might be on the wolves' side for now, but not everyone was happy. That was why he and Dhani had mated the way they had. And though the whole show had been because some humans weren't happy, Kameron wasn't sure any of it had been for a good reason. Because now, some were reporting that Dhani was in danger by being with him. Or at least being near the Pack. Some didn't believe that she was mated in—or *married* as some reporters called it since they refused to use the term *mating*. And still others were calling for her to be taken out of the equation completely.

Not necessarily death, but hidden away from anything that could be attached to the paranormal. Her parents had been quiet on the media front for the past couple of days, but their initial pleading to have their baby girl back was on rotation on some news sites. And that meant that everything was still fucked up. Because it had been the humans who attacked them, at least from what he could tell by scent. He wasn't sure about the magic. Wasn't sure about anything honestly, but he had scented human.

"Hey, boss, you're going to want to see this." Tino came in and turned on the TV that was in Kameron's office. Dave was right behind Tino, a fierce expression on his face as he folded his arms over his chest.

"Shit." Kameron pinched the bridge of his nose, forcing his wolf back so he didn't growl or slash at his desk.

The news anchor went on and on about the proposed note that had been sent to them from the human contingent that was against the wolves. They didn't have a proper name or title yet, but Kameron knew it was coming. All terrorist organizations had a distinction, even if it was one made up by the media. And that's what this contingent was. A terrorist organization. According to them, they knew that the human women attached to the wolves were not safe.

And they said they would stop at nothing to make sure they were safe. They hadn't come out and taken responsibility for the bomb, but they might as well have. The media had alluded to it.

Because the ramifications of that act were on the human side. And Kameron was pissed.

"We're going to need to talk to Gideon because I have no idea what to do next. Because this isn't just a rival Pack attacking us. This isn't just the paranormal. Now, we're getting into politics and humans and everything that doesn't have anything to do with us. But in the end, they tried to hurt my mate. So if I don't talk to Gideon and have my Alpha calm me down, I'm going to fucking kill someone right now."

"Then let's go to the house. We can get the family there —or at least some of them." Max started tidying up his notes while Kameron looked over at Tino and Dave. They weren't part of the upper hierarchy but were still part of Kameron's team. He trusted them, probably more than he trusted anyone outside of his immediate family. They had always been there, had always protected Dhani even when she had just been coming into the den to visit her friends. They'd always been there to watch over her when Kameron didn't know she was his mate. Because it had taken a while after meeting her for the mating bonds to be fixed so they could even feel that tug, that pull.

And that meant he trusted the two men with his mate, part of his soul.

He would do his best to make sure they understood that,

even if he was so damn angry right now he couldn't put it into words.

"I know you guys have patrol today before you head out for sentry duty to keep on the lookout. I'll keep you guys in the loop once we figure out what's going on. Thanks for letting me know about the broadcast. I probably would've heard about it later, but I'm glad you guys are keeping me up-to-date."

Tino raised his chin. "No problem, Kameron. I don't particularly like the fact that they're using Dhani as their symbol when her community was the one that pushed her out in the first place."

"We'll take care of her," Dave added. Then the two men walked out of the office, and Kameron and Max followed soon after.

Kameron texted Gideon as he walked, only bumping into a couple of people who were also texting and walking. Usually, others gave him a wide berth, inherently avoiding him when it came to his wolf and his position. But, apparently, mating Dhani had changed things. He still wasn't quite sure if he liked that. People needed to be slightly afraid of him for him to protect them properly. He was going to have to find that balance again. He just hoped Dhani understood.

And there it was again, him putting her first. He knew that's what he needed to do, but it was still weird not putting the Pack and their safety above all else. He would just have to get used to it like he had been getting used to everything recently.

His brother was already at the front of the house, the door open, when Max and Kameron made their way to Gideon's. His Alpha didn't look happy, of course. He never did these days unless he had his baby or his mate in his arms.

"Come inside. It's just the three of us for now because the others are all working or on their own patrols. We'll let them know what happens, but we need to figure out what the fuck we're going to do. Because no matter how many times I take a stand, it's not working. And the idea of having to hurt someone in order for them to take us seriously...I know it's going to make things worse in the end. Frankly, I don't like the fact that we don't have any true evidence about who attacked us yet again. Because this time it wasn't magic, despite the fact that you think you might have scented it."

"I can't tell you for sure. It could've just been a trace of the wards or another witch. It's not like we can truly figure out the difference between each witch these days. It takes a witch to know exactly what kind of magic is being used, and that's not something I can do. I know that we have more witches in our soldier ranks now as our Pack grows stronger, but it's not enough. And at this point, I'm not certain it'll ever be enough."

"And I thought I was the pessimist," Max said quietly from his side.

Kameron flipped him off, and it was a testament to Gideon's frayed nerves that his brother didn't say anything or even flip Max off, too.

"Even if there was a touch of magic, there were humans here. That means that humans hurt my mate. And it's taking everything within me now not to go after them. Not to make them aware that they can't attack us again. Not to prove that we are the nightmares they fear."

Gideon gave him a look, and the three of them talked about what was to come and the threat. The entire time, his brother and Alpha never gave him the order not to attack those who dared to hurt his mate. Because Gideon shouldn't have to. Kameron was the Enforcer, he wasn't supposed to make stupid moves like that.

But he was afraid if he weren't careful, he might just break everything that he'd built because *no one* was allowed to hurt what was his.

And though he had tried to run from it, though he'd tried to find another way, Dhani was his. And he would protect her. No matter the cost.

CHAPTER EIGHTEEN

Dhani yawned as they walked into their bedroom. She was still getting used to calling it *theirs* rather than his, but she was making a choice to actively put herself into this new life instead of passively letting it pass her by. Kameron ran his hand along her hip before giving it a pat.

"Are you tired? We can head to bed if you want. I can look over some notes while you sleep."

She stopped walking and looked up at him. "Really? That sounds so domestic."

He shrugged. "We're in the middle of a shadow and political war. My mate's tired, and I have work to do. I don't mind sounding domestic if it means you get some sleep."

Yes, she was falling for this man. No...she'd already fallen for him.

And times like these just proved it. How had she thought

that Kameron was standoffish? He might play the icy Enforcer, but there were so many layers to him that it was hard for her to keep up.

"You know...I'm not that tired."

He smiled down at her. "Oh, really?"

"Really. I mean, we've probably worn out the bed at this point, but for a man who claims he likes it rough and wants to rock my world, you haven't taken me against the wall yet. Or the door. Or on a table. Or—"

She didn't have time to finish her sentence because Kameron's mouth was on hers, and his claws—his actual claws—were tearing off her clothes. Then her back was against the door, and she was tugging on his shirt. Somehow, he was able to hold her up with one hand to strip off his clothes, as well. Thank the goddess for shifters and their strength and claws.

When he slid into her with one thrust, she actually came. Just like that. She would have been embarrassed, but Kameron was fucking her too hard, too fast into the door for her to find the emotion.

Instead, she dug her nails into his back, knowing she was breaking the skin, knowing he liked it from the way his glowing eyes met hers.

"Hard enough?" he growled.

"It's everything," she said honestly. What more was there to say?

"Play with yourself. Make yourself come, and then we'll go to our boring bed, and I'll fuck you again."

She bent forward and bit his lip, loving the way he

grinned. "There's nothing boring about you, Kameron. And you know it."

"Damn straight."

Then he made her come.

Again.

And again.

And as they lay in each other's arms afterward, she knew that Kameron was almost asleep, and that was why she felt as if she could say the words. The words she knew she could keep to herself even though, deep inside, her soul already knew the answer.

"I love you," she whispered. She loved his strength, his humor, his ice. She loved him.

But he didn't answer.

And because she could hear the deep sounds of his breath, the slight growl he made in his sleep, she wasn't sure he'd heard her. But that was just as well because she wasn't sure she could bear to hear the answer to those words—if there was one. The time would come, she knew. But until then, she would be his mate, be a part of the Pack, and try to find her place in this new world.

Love or not, she was his, and he was hers.

She'd just have to figure out what to do about that.

THE DREAM HIT her hard again, and she screamed out at the shock, but she knew this time it wasn't aloud. Kameron wouldn't wake her until the dream wanted her to be woken up. Flames danced on her skin, but this time, she wasn't alone.

Aimee and Dawn faced her, their wrists in chains as they stared at her, their mouths opened wide in silent screams. They reached for her, but Dhani couldn't move from her spot. Cheyenne was there, too, in shadow, not a part of things but not separate. Just there.

Dhani blinked, and the scene changed.

The old woman stood between her friends now. Her arms outstretched and her palms facing outward. She mumbled something Dhani couldn't understand, but she knew it was important. Knew it had been said before.

Stand up.

Open up.

Give up.

Sacrifice begets sacrifice.

Her friends screamed after the woman had finished speaking, and Dhani screamed with them. Then she found herself awake in her bed, Kameron's arms tight around her as he nuzzled her neck over the mating mark he'd placed there.

Something was coming. Soon, the dreams wouldn't be of what was to come but what was already here.

If only she had a clue how to decipher what the words meant.

HOURS LATER, she was finishing up an afternoon lesson while her pups—she was still getting used to calling them that rather than *kids*—smiled and chatted as if they didn't have a care in the world. And for them, perhaps that was the case. That was how it should be. Dhani wished she were able to think like they did but, for some reason, her sense of knowing seemed to hit her full force and she was having trouble concentrating.

Her hands shook every once in a while as she tried to finish her lessons, and her heart raced even when she thought she was finally calming down. There was something approaching, something bad, and she knew if she weren't careful, the innocent children in front of her would be in the line of fire.

Yet she didn't know why she kept thinking those horrible thoughts. Because these babies needed to be safe when they were inside the den wards. That was the whole point of having them cloistered inside them, after all. There were maternal dominants, dominants, submissives, soldiers, and every other kind of wolf and witch out there, ready to defend their territory and the children with their lives. And she knew it probably wouldn't even come to that because it would take a lot of magic and pain for them to reach this part of the den at all. But she still had a bad feeling about her presence there and had no idea what she was going to do about it. She had no idea why she felt this way. Maybe it was just a bad dream that she couldn't quite wake up from. Or maybe it was just a feeling that had nothing to do with the children finishing up their lessons in front of her.

When one of them raised their tiny hand to ask a question, she pushed those thoughts out of her head and did what she was supposed to do. Her new role in this new life of hers was to take care of these children and teach them. She didn't have time to stand around and wonder about the what-ifs and be scared all the time.

She trusted her mate and his people to protect the borders. She trusted the wards around them, even if they made her skin prickle more than anyone else's. So she just needed to get over what was bothering her and actually focus on her job. Because there weren't as many children in this school as there were in the human one, and she could focus on each child individually as much as possible.

School days were split up into half days with one grade in the morning and one grade in the afternoon. When the students weren't in their actual homeroom, they were either at daycare or taking lessons from someone else. It was as close to a one-room school as they could get without forcing the younger children to learn lessons that were too hard or not teaching the older children enough. As the Pack grew and more babies were born, things would change. Apparently, the den had already changed drastically in the past few years.

There were far more children under the age of twelve than there were older kids, and that was because of the timing of the new matings when the Talon Pack had started to heal.

There was so much history surrounding the people around her, and she just wanted to soak it all up and learn as much as she could. And not just because she wanted to learn more about her mate.

As she helped the kids finish up the last of their lessons and then walked them to the next part of their day, she found herself standing alone by the building that had taken her in, thinking about Kameron. She had been thinking about him a lot. She'd told him that she loved him, yet she was pretty sure he hadn't heard her. That was probably for the best because she honestly didn't think they would have been anywhere near this point in their relationship if they were human. Of course, she was *still* human, but she could feel this magical pulse inside her, telling her that she was mated to someone who wasn't human.

It should have been weird, but it felt right. It felt as if she were finally holding onto something that she'd been missing for far too long. The thing was, she wasn't sure all of that feeling came from Kameron or if it was just the magic itself. She was really starting to wonder if maybe this sense of knowing of hers, the way she reacted to the wards, and the way she felt at home with people who celebrated magic was part of some bigger picture. But she had no idea if that was true or what it all meant.

She hated feeling as if she didn't have a clue what she was doing, yet that seemed to be happening more often than not recently. She was still learning, still trying to get all the facts and trying to fit in. And though things had changed drastically since she was on the outside looking in, she knew she was still missing something. Was that something Kameron? Because she *had* him now. She could feel that he cared for her. He was different around her. Different than he had been when he was walking around shirtless and growling before. Now, he walked shirtless and growled for a whole different reason. And that growl did something completely different to her than it had, something she really liked. Who knew she'd like growling that much?

Now, her mind was going in a thousand different directions because everything was hitting her at once. She still couldn't reach her parents, and she wasn't sure she wanted to. What if the others were wrong and Blade had nothing to do with this? What if Aspen was just a last name, and Blade hadn't had any contact with her parents. Or maybe the other man had reached out, but her parents were willingly going along with him and his plans and schemes. But…what if they were in danger and she couldn't help them? Though Kameron had two of his men watching her mom and dad, they hadn't been able to get too close for fear of what would happen if they did. So now she felt as if she were cut off from the only two people she'd had before she met Aimee, Dawn, and Cheyenne.

Her relationship with her parents might be strained, but that was on the three of them, not just her parents. She was just as much at fault for the tenuous lines of communication they shared. There'd always been something missing, something that had nothing to do with who they were, who *she* was. It had everything to do with the lack of something, but she'd never been able to figure out exactly what it was.

And now she couldn't talk to them. Couldn't see them. She was still so angry about their words, even if they hadn't been the ones in charge of what they said. Those words and what came as a result of them was what kept the pups in her classroom in danger.

Somehow, she still felt far out of the loop, so very behind. The past week, she had spent almost all of her time either teaching or with Kameron. Because even though they had mated in order to keep the den safe, she figured that everyone knew she and Kameron needed some time alone to figure out who they were together. And that was how she had fallen for him so fast. Or, at least it was part of it. He was a different person now that she could see beneath his layers. She just didn't know if he realized that.

Or maybe he did, and he didn't like it.

Because her thoughts were annoying her, she was glad that she was headed to Dawn's house as soon as she left the classroom. Aimee would be there as well, and they had smuggled in Cheyenne. Cheyenne had been forced to stay away from the den and everyone for far too long because no one wanted her to be seen as being too connected to them. Somehow, her name had been left out of the press, but Dhani knew that wouldn't last long. So they had hidden her in the back of an SUV to get her into the den for girls' night. Cheyenne probably wasn't too happy about that since the woman liked to fight things head-on, but her friend also wanted to keep the innocents safe. She cared for those who couldn't care for themselves. That was how she lived, how she breathed.

And despite how Dhani felt sometimes, she and Cheyenne were still human. They were the weakest of the bunch, and somehow they needed to toe the line and listen to what everyone else said about safety and danger. It didn't make the pill of having to bow down any easier to swallow.

And while Dhani understood that, she was really afraid that Cheyenne might start to distance herself even more. Because Cheyenne had no connection to the den. No connection to the people inside other than friendship. One day, Dhani would be a shifter, just like the others. And when that happened, she would cease to age. Aimee, Dawn, and Dhani would grow into this new world of shifters and paranormal and slowly separate themselves from the human one. Yes, the whole idea of their Pack at this time and this moment was to integrate themselves with humans, but there was still a distance. Because humans aged and died. Shifters didn't. And that meant, one day, they would have to say goodbye to Cheyenne. And Dhani was really afraid that Cheyenne would be the one to say goodbye first.

So that was why she was happy that Cheyenne would be there today. She missed her friend. She missed talking to all three of them, frankly. She had so many thoughts her head, and she needed to get them out, and Dhani knew her friends could help. Because that's what friends were for, and her friends were some of the best out there. They not only kicked ass but they also listened when someone needed to vent. And she had a lot she needed to vent about.

But most importantly, she needed to tell her friends about the *knowing* that was growing increasingly hard to ignore.

Something was coming.

And she needed to tell someone before it was too late.

BY THE TIME she made it to Dawn's place, Dhani was practically shaking with anticipation and worry. She missed her circle, her girls, and knew she needed to tell them everything that had happened, even if she didn't understand it herself.

"What's wrong?" Amiee asked as soon as Dhani walked into the house. Her friend had piled her long, blond hair up on top of her head, but she had worry in her gaze. Her friend was so strong, so much stronger than she was even a month ago. Changing into a lion shifter truly looked good on Dhani's best friend.

Cheyenne was sitting on the couch, her eyes narrowing as she studied Dhani. And Dawn was just walking into the living room, a plate of mini tacos in her hand. Apparently, they were going to snack while Dhani broke down. Of course, the girls were there to talk about everything, but Dhani had a feeling she wouldn't be able to hold back for long. And since Aimee had opened the door with the question, Dhani wasn't going to hold back at all.

"I think I need to leave the den." She hadn't known the words were going to come out of her mouth until they had. But now that they were out, she knew they were the right ones. She couldn't be in the den anymore. Something was coming, and it was going to surround her. She wasn't so self-centered to think it would only be about her, but she knew...she *knew* that if she stayed inside of the den wards, others would be hurt because of her. She wasn't saying that others wouldn't be hurt at all, but more people would be safe if she was away. Just thinking that hurt. Because this place was her new home. She finally felt like she actually belonged, but now she knew that if she stayed, things would get bad.

And the fact that her friends only stared at her, and they didn't look at her as if she were crazy, told her how close to the edge she truly was. Because they had gotten used to her knowing things, even if they never said anything about it. Even if *she* had never said anything about it.

She was scared. So damn scared. Terrified of losing everything that she had just found. Of losing Kameron. And she had no idea why all these feelings were hitting her then, but it was important. And it was important that she not stay; that she leave and find someplace to be safe outside of the den. She didn't want the babies to die because of her. Because she knew if she stayed, they would be hurt. Just the images that came to mind when she thought that made her want to throw up.

Maybe she truly was going insane, but if she stayed, she would only go further past the brink.

"You're going to have to explain things a little slower. Or give us details." Dawn came forward after setting down the plate of mini tacos. Her friend held her close, but Dhani stood straight, stiff, afraid that if she were to move just then, she'd break before she explained everything.

"You know I always have these...feelings." She had no idea what she was going to say to explain, but she had to get her friends to believe her.

"We do." Aimee gave Cheyenne a look when their friend frowned, looking as if she didn't actually believe what was going on. Dhani didn't blame Cheyenne since she knew she sounded crazy.

"I've always had this...knowing. This idea that I was meant to be something more. And it wasn't just because I didn't like my job or my place in my family. All of that was part of it, but it wasn't all of it. I finally feel like I'm where I'm supposed to be. At least in the grand scheme of things. Kameron is my mate, and though we went into this a little quicker than we would've liked, I know that I'm supposed to be with him. I know I'm supposed to be inside this den and part of this Pack. But I also know that I need to leave it for a time. I need to keep others safe by not being here. Because I think that bomb was meant for me. Kameron got hurt because of me."

Dawn shook her head. "No. It's not your fault that Kameron got hurt. It's not your fault that this human contingent or whatever they're calling themselves these days thinks that you're a symbol for them. It's not your fault that they don't understand that we don't walk their night-mares and take out children. It's not your fault. You are a human living amongst shifters, and for some reason, you're a symbol of what they think is wrong with the world. But they are wrong."

Cheyenne stood up and slowly walked her way towards the others. "You need to go." She held up her hands when the others protested, and Dhani was grateful. The other two in the room might be shifters, but she and Cheyenne were the hardest of the four. Always had been. Aimee and Dawn were strong, they had to be, but they were also softer in ways that came from their hearts. And while Dhani tried that, sometimes, she was just a little more jagged than the other two. Hence why she fit with Kameron so well despite the fact that he hadn't thought they would.

Cheyenne met Dhani's gaze and continued. "You know I don't usually believe in all the magic-rules-the-world crap, but I'm surrounded by it and have been forced to face the fact that science and everything I thought was the only true way, isn't. We've always known that there was something off about you. Not weird, but different. Just like we knew that there was something different about Dawn. Something wrong with Aimee. We all knew, and we didn't say anything because we were so worried about what others might think or because we thought that everything would be okay because we had each other. But all of you have been hurt because of that. All of you. I don't want that to happen again. If you think that you need to be outside of the den to keep others safe, Dhani, you should trust that feeling. Maybe you'll figure out why it is that way, maybe you'll figure out the connection. Or maybe you won't. But if you've been listening to that gut feeling of yours this whole time while trying to find your place...then you need to follow it now. Talk to Kameron. Find a safe place and hide. I don't know what's coming. I don't know much of anything anymore. I don't feel like I'm connected to anything anymore, and maybe that's okay. Maybe that's *my* gut feeling. But I want you safe. Because even if I don't understand where all of you are going, you're my best friends. And I'll love you until the end of time. Even if my time seems to be a bit shorter."

Tears were freely falling down everyone's faces by then, and Dhani held her friends close, knowing that things were about to change again. But something was coming. That prophecy of the words in her head wasn't going away. If anything, it was echoing even louder with each ebb and flow. That meant that she had to find Kameron. Had to tell him exactly what was coming. Or at least what must be done.

She just hoped he believed her.

Because she didn't know what she would do with herself if he got hurt again because of her. She honestly didn't know what she would do if *anyone* got hurt because of her. And while her friends might be right and the fault landed on the ones that harmed them, some part of her knew that she had been part of the reason for all of it. It was time for her to make a move.

She just had to talk to her mate first.

CHAPTER NINETEEN

Kameron had a feeling he wasn't going to like what Dhani had to say to him, but he could feel the terror along the mating bond, and that worried him, too. Because it wasn't about what was going on around her at that very moment, it was about something that was going to happen in the future. He had no idea why he knew that, but he had a feeling it had to do with the woman on the other end of his mating bond, and not him.

He knew she wasn't *just* human. There was something different about her, and they needed to figure it out.

But first, it seemed, he was going to have to see what she had to say. And he knew he wouldn't like it.

"You're shaking. I only scent your friends on you, so I'm going to take it that something's wrong inside and not that something's coming to attack you. Because if you need me to rough someone up, I will. All you have to do is ask."

"You say that, but I feel like I'm going crazy. There's something wrong. Something imminent. And I've said those two phrases so many times, I don't even know what they mean anymore."

He cupped her cheeks, bringing his face closer to hers. His wolf was on edge, digging from the inside, clawing at him to do something. He might be a shifter, might turn into a wolf even without the call of the moon, but he still hated all the magical bullshit. He hated that there wasn't something tactile, something tangible for his hands to tear apart. He'd always been that way when it came to protecting his family and his Pack. And now that he had Dhani in his life, it was even more so.

"Just tell me. I'm ready to try and figure it out with you. But if you keep it all bottled up inside, there's nothing I can do." He knew the irony of those words since he was the one who tended to bottle everything up and not let anyone know what was going on with him, but he didn't want that for Dhani. Everything had come at her so quickly. He still felt as if *he* were trying to catch up, and he knew that she must feel even further behind.

So he was going to listen to what she told him, and then he was going to hope to the goddess that he could fix it for her.

Because that was who he was. He was the fixer. The protector. And if he couldn't do that, especially with his mate, he didn't know what his purpose was at all.

"You know those dreams I've been having? Well, they're coming more and more frequently. To the point that I'm not even screaming in reality when I wake up so I'm not waking you. I feel like I'm getting used to them. And I shouldn't get used to them. And, yes, I know I should've woken you up, but I couldn't. I needed to figure out what they were. I keep dreaming about this old woman telling me very specific words. I don't know what they mean, but I know that they're important. If you add that into the feeling of *knowing*, I just know I need to leave the den."

He let out a growl. Yeah, he didn't like what she was saying one bit. He was going to have to circle back to that whole not waking him thing, as well. Because he was done with that shit. If she didn't trust him with her dreams, how could she trust him when she was awake?

"Not forever," she added when he didn't say anything. She put her hand on his arm, his wolf bucking at her touch, and continued. "I promise you. I know I can't be here when the next hurdle we have to jump comes at us. I know I have to be somewhere away from those pups and the innocent when whoever is out to get the Talons comes again. And I know it doesn't make any sense. I know I don't have any evidence of this deep feeling of wrongness. But I hope you believe me because I have to leave even if I don't get your help. But I need your help, Kameron. I need you. I'm so sorry."

Kameron was the quiet one, the one that didn't ramble. He was one who growled and got shit done. But right then, all he wanted to do was hold her close. How in the hell did this happen to them? Out of the four friends that had come to the Talons, he'd always assumed that Dhani was the most rational and serious of the bunch. Yes, Cheyenne was rational and very scientific. But she also tended to go on tangents when she wanted to figure out exactly how things worked. Dhani was always the sarcastic one that got shit done—just like he did.

The fact that she was so rattled about what was coming told him that something was indeed wrong. Something was indeed coming. And he was going to have to figure out how to fix it for her. Even if that meant taking her outside the safety of the den.

Even thinking that made his stomach roll. But if that's what she needed, that's what he would do.

Even if it hurt him, even if it killed him a little.

"I believe you. You need to remember that I am constantly surrounded by magic. I've lived in this world for over a century. I've witnessed foreseers in the middle of a thrall. Spoken to elders that watched civilizations fall and rise again. My brother, my triplet, heals with his hands. The other heals emotions with just his soul. I can feel every single person that is connected to this Pack. I have individual bonds with every single person, just like my Alpha does. They're not as strong, and I have to focus on that if I want to truly know which person is which, but because of those bonds, I know when there is something coming. I know when there's an outside force about to get my Pack. I grew up believing that. And I believe you. Frankly, I kept thinking that this sense of urgency just came from our mating bond, but maybe I was wrong. Maybe it's because you're you and I'm the Enforcer that I totally believe you.

My bonds are telling me that I need to make sure you're safe. Need to *keep* you safe. Because I believe you. Of course, I do. I'm not happy about it. Not happy that you're in danger. And I'll kill anybody that comes after you. You understand me? Because you're mine. You're stuck with me until the end of our days, and those days better last a long fucking time."

He kissed her hard, not knowing if it was the right thing to do, but he and his wolf needed her taste. When she sank into him, he knew that she needed the reassurance, as well. She might not be a wolf yet, but she needed the tactile touch just as much as he did.

He was still learning how to be a mate, how to be a man who protected the one closest to him as much as he protected the others, but he was learning. Slowly. At least he wished it were a little slower considering that everything was falling down around them once again and he was having to move pretty damn fast just to do the right thing.

"I don't know where to go. I don't know what to do. And I hate that because I always have a plan."

Kameron frowned, trying to think about what holdings he had in place for weird emergencies like this. They didn't always have to hide their Pack members outside of the den, but there had been enough issues over the past decade or so that Kameron had safe houses just in case. He didn't want to take her to the closest one just in case it wasn't far enough away, but he had one about twenty minutes away that might work for her. When he told her about the small cabin, her eyes went wide, and she nodded. Now he just had to get two of his most trusted men on board to protect her. Because he couldn't leave the Pack alone, and he sure as hell wasn't leaving his mate alone.

"Go inside and pack a few things. Don't make the bag too large. Just enough so it looks like we're going on a hiking trip." He trusted those in his Pack, but then again, he'd trusted the ones who betrayed the Pack before. However, he was more worried about someone watching them leave the wards. They needed the world to think that he and Dhani were leaving the den just for a little bit, therefore keeping those inside safe. But they also had to hide their trail along the way so the humans didn't know where he and Dhani ended up.

It wouldn't be easy, but this was what he did. As Dhani walked inside, he pulled out his phone and dialed Tino. Between Dave and Tino, his mate would be safe. He trusted them with his life; therefore, he trusted them with his mate.

And Kameron didn't trust easily.

He could've called any of his brothers or cousins to protect her, but he didn't want to pull them away from their mates or their duties. And while Max could fight anyone, his cousin was too busy working on the notes and trails for Blade. He didn't want to split his cousin's focus so, therefore, the two sentries who might one day be true soldiers like Max would have to do.

By the time he and Dhani were at the cabin, Gideon and the rest of the Brentwoods knew exactly what was happening even if they didn't understand Kameron's urgency. They didn't understand his mate, but they trusted him, and they trusted her. And all of them had been through enough themselves to know that when it felt as if the moon goddess were pushing you to do something, you listened. She was their goddess for a reason. And he had a feeling she wasn't done making sure her people knew she was still a presence.

Tino and Dave were already at the cabin, checking for security threats and getting ready for his mate to be there. He didn't totally like the idea that he had to leave Dhani there with his two soldiers, but he couldn't stay by her side the whole time. And Dhani understood that. Because he needed to protect the Pack, and he couldn't do that outside the den wards for long. For a man who had his own balance of magic with actual science and data, relying on his bonds as an Enforcer and the magic around them—even though they were outside the den wards because of magic —wasn't an easy thing to process. But he was getting it done.

Both of his soldiers were outside the cabin, patiently waiting for Kameron to leave. The two knew he wanted a few more minutes with his mate.

He kissed her softly, his wolf growling at him. He didn't want to leave, but his Alpha had given him a mission, and he needed to follow through. He couldn't betray Gideon by staying with Dhani, and he couldn't bring his mate with him either. He hated every bit of their current situation.

"You need to go, or you're going to miss out on an opportunity."

He'd told her about the off times of the building he and

his cousin were going to check out as part of the mission, but he wished there was another way to go about it.

She kissed his chin, and his wolf pushed him again. It wanted him to mark her right there and then, making sure everyone knew whom she belonged to, whom he belonged to, but this wasn't the time or place. Yet.

"I'll go when I'm ready. You know Cheyenne's coming over a little bit later, that way, you're not all alone with these two guys. I don't know how she convinced everyone else to let her come to the cabin when she could be in danger, too, but I'm glad you won't be alone. Stay inside, be safe. But if you need me, I'll be here. Even if I have to run full-tilt for miles, I will be right here."

"I know. I know it's weird that we're here instead of safely inside the wards, but even Avery, as a foreseer, agreed that I need to stay away from the innocent right now." Avery had let that morsel drop right as the two of them were leaving their house. His sister-in-law was growing into her powers, and thankfully, her mates were able to keep her steady because he knew that much magic and power at once had to be hard on her. Parker and Brandon were watching out for her, though, and for that he was grateful.

Dhani continued, "We both know that Tino and Dave have watched out for me since the beginning, and as you said, Cheyenne will be here as well to make sure nothing happens. She might be human just like me, but I'm pretty sure she could take a whole army with just her medical bag."

Since he believed her about Cheyenne, he didn't

comment. But he did lower his head and kiss her softly. His wolf didn't want to be away from her. Neither did the man. But he didn't have a choice. Gideon needed him to complete this mission, and he needed to make sure that the women who were part of his world—Dhani and Cheyenne, and any other human ever attached to the Talon Pack—were safe. The Pack had won the war against the demon years ago and had won the war against the humans who were out to get them after. They had fought against politics and laws in some cases, and fangs and claws in others. They had bled on the battlefield, as well as in legislature.

But now, they were fighting an enemy who didn't come at them head-on. He knew that Blade was somehow responsible for everything that was going on, but that didn't mean the smaller pieces weren't at fault, as well. So Kameron would go where he needed to and take care of what was required. And then he would come back to his mate and ensure that she was safe.

He had a feeling they wouldn't be waiting long for her transformation into a wolf because he knew she hated hiding away and not being able to fight. And he didn't like the idea that she didn't have another form of defense. Her only option was hiding or using others around her to do the fighting for her. And that wasn't something that either of them liked.

So now she would be forced to lose her humanity because of the humans who may be out to get her, and for sure because of Blade.

Kameron knew that the Aspens would need to be

stopped soon. And even though the Talons and the Redwoods weren't strong enough to fight them head-on, it wouldn't matter in the end. They were still losing, and that wasn't something he and his family would ever allow for too long, no matter the sacrifice.

So he kissed his mate again and pressed his forehead to hers. "Stay inside. Be safe. Don't do anything stupid. I only say that because *I* might do something stupid to protect you, and I don't want that to happen either."

She raised her brow, her mouth twitching as if she were holding back a smile. "So don't be stupid."

He was the one who smiled then, and then he said something he should have said before this even though he hadn't known he was feeling it. He wasn't good at telling people what he felt, wasn't good at saying anything in general usually. But there was something inside him now, something along the bond that told him if he didn't say it now, there might not be another chance. And though that worried him, he wouldn't let it stop him either.

"I love you. So don't be stupid."

Her eyes widened before she rolled them. "That was... oddly romantic and *so* us. I love you too, my big, bad wolf. But please be safe. I'm the one hiding behind these walls, but you'll be out dealing with what you need to take care of. I know things are moving fast—they always are it seems with us—but I kind of like that we're at where we're at... once we're both safe that is." She paused, and he ran his thumb along her cheek.

"What?"

"I kind of already told you that I love you, but I think you were sleeping so I don't know if that counts. I don't want you to think that I said the words just because you did, because I've been thinking them for a while, but I also thought that we were moving too fast. And you know I don't like feeling that way. You know I don't like feeling as if I'm only doing things because fate tells me to. Because that's not the case. I just wanted you to know that. So be safe, don't be stupid, come back to me. Because once you do, maybe we can figure out how to do this whole relationship thing on our own terms instead of letting fate and wolves and enemies dictate it. Because I like you. I love you. I want to figure out our path. Together."

"I didn't know you said it before, but I'm glad you said it now," he whispered before kissing her.

While his wolf wanted to once again mark her, he knew there would be time for that later. Because there had to be. That was the whole reason they were going along with this plan, even if part of him knew that it might not work. So he kissed her again, made sure she was safe, and left. Tino and Dave would take care of her, he knew that.

He just hated relying on anyone but himself.

Gideon had asked him to go to the human contingent and talk. He'd found that odd since he wasn't the diplomat of the family. He was the one that got shit done. He was the one they called in if they needed something to get bloody. Because that was his role, and it was one he relished. But maybe his brother had thought that because Kameron was fighting for a mate now and not just himself and his Pack, things would be different. He wasn't sure, but he was going to find out.

Max and Ryder had figured out where the human contingent's headquarters was located, and now Kameron was going to stealthily get there and see what he could find out. He wasn't going to lay waste to the area and kill everyone—even if part of him wanted to. He was just going to talk and gather information with Max by his side.

The two of them would hold each other back from destroying everything.

Hopefully.

Max met Kameron at the edge of the road, and he jumped into his cousin's car. They drove silently towards the coordinates they had, no words needing to be spoken. He and Max weren't all that talkative anyway.

They drove up to a building that had a plain front and a sign that just said it was a commercial property. There was no business name listed. No indication that inside was a human contingent that was out to get all shifters and witches and anything not their kind of normal. It wasn't as if Kam had really been expecting that, but everything looked a little too...ordinary for him. It all looked a little too plain. Nothing looked as if it were the headquarters for a group ready to set up a strategic defense or offense against the paranormal. It honestly looked like a paper pushing building. But maybe that was their goal, to make it look like they were one thing when really, they were another.

Or maybe they *were* paper pushers, and this was all

Blade. Kameron hated the fact that he didn't know, but since he and Max were there, he was going to find out.

They parked off to the side where they would be outside of camera range and any other defensive things the humans might have in place. Slowly, the two of them worked their way around the building, taking mental notes while Max took photos. They needed to find out who this group was and what their agenda was. And that meant it was time for Kameron to be the diplomat. Something he really didn't want to be.

He walked right up to the front, not scenting any gun oil or hearing the whir of any cameras on him. He honestly had no idea what the hell this group was doing, but either they had the best security, or possibly the worst. Max was still hiding just in case Kameron needed backup, but for some strange reason, Kameron didn't think he would need his cousin.

The door opened, and a man in khaki pants and a polo shirt stood there, his eyes wide, and his hand tightening around the edge of the door. He didn't look armed; in fact, Kameron wasn't sure the man would even know how to hold a gun. Then again, it was a bomb someone had used against them, not a gun. Something didn't smell right, though. Something was off.

And it had nothing to do with bombs or guns and everything to do with the information they had.

"You're Kameron, the Enforcer," the other man stuttered as he spoke, the fear wafting off of him pungent.

Kam wasn't surprised that he'd been recognized. The

world knew who the Talons were, even if his people tried to keep their children and some of the lower-profile wolves hidden for their safety.

Kameron raised his chin, and the other man didn't bother meeting his eyes. There was no need when there clearly wasn't a dominance battle going on.

The other man continued since Kameron didn't say anything. He didn't need to. Not yet.

"I don't know if you can scent it or not, but I'm all alone here. We're not working today. We mean you no harm."

Kameron barely held back a snort.

"We just want information. We want to know how you guys came to be, and why you're here. Since you're here now, can you talk to me? Can I put you on record and can you tell me more about the paranormals? Because we don't want to harm you. We just want to understand. We want to know why we're not allowed on Talon territory. We want to know everything. Because we don't want to be what those other people were in the past, the ones who came at you with violence. That's not our goal. We just don't understand. So can you sit and talk to me?"

Kameron stood there, listening to this man ramble, and knew that he was in the wrong place. These guys might be problematic and might one day be dangerous if they looked too far into things that they didn't understand, but they weren't the ones who set off the bomb. He didn't think they were smart enough to do that. Maybe they were smart, but just in a bookish way. There was something else going on, and it all had to do with the Pack Alpha of the Aspens.

He'd known it before, but he'd let that scent at the edge of the compound and the media sway him.

And he was wrong. So he was going to make sure this man and his people had nothing to do with the bomb before he left. The Talons wouldn't let this group become a threat, but Kameron needed facts.

"You weren't the ones who set off the bomb on Pack territory."

It wasn't a question, but the man answered anyway. He put his hands up in front of him in surrender and shook his head, his face going pale.

"No, of course not. We aren't violent. We just think, no… we *know* we have a right to know what's going on up there. But that bomb wasn't us. We would never hurt you guys. I have pamphlets and papers and everything to tell you our goals. There are some on the news that are little more vocal, but even they don't want violence. They just want peace. They want knowledge. They want to know who you are."

Kameron growled and turned on his heel, leaving the other man sputtering behind him. He jumped into the car as Max started driving off. He didn't need to tell his cousin that he was done with this shit. Because Max probably heard everything, and Kameron needed to get back to his mate. Because they had gone on a wild goose chase for nothing. These humans hadn't done anything. They were annoying, sure, and might pose a problem soon, but they weren't the ones who attacked his mate. They hadn't been the ones to put her parents on live television to try and incite a riot. That had been Blade. That much Kameron knew for sure. And he had left his mate alone. She might be surrounded by two of his best men and her friend, but she was still alone because he wasn't there.

He just hoped that he hadn't made a big fucking mistake.

He growled, called in an update to Gideon and the others, and tried not to tear into the car as Max drove. As soon as he got off the phone with Gideon, his phone rang, and chills broke out over his skin and ran down his spine.

He picked up the phone and answered with a growl. "Cheyenne. Where's Dhani?"

"I was just calling to ask the same damn thing. Because she's not here. Where the fuck is she? There's blood on the ground, and I think...I think Tino is dead." She let out a curse but Kameron held his in. "He doesn't have a pulse, but for all I know, you guys can come back from an injury like this. You need to get here. Because Dave isn't here, and there's blood everywhere. Dhani isn't here, Kameron. Where is she?"

Kameron let out a howl that he knew others would be able to hear from miles away, and Max didn't even swerve at the noise. His cousin just slammed his foot down on the gas pedal and sped their way to the cabin. Kam knew they would get there, but not in time.

Tino was dead.

Dave was missing.

Dhani was missing.

And Kameron was going to murder anybody who dared to harm her. No matter the cost.

CHAPTER TWENTY

Dhani's head hurt, and she felt as if she had been submerged underwater, drowned, then knocked upside the head with a rock. Considering that she didn't really remember how she ended up where she was, that might have been exactly what happened.

She groaned, forced herself into a seated position, and looked around her. To her right was just a stone wall with water trickling down it, and in front of her was the same, only with a little more space. She seemed to be in a corner of something like a basement, but she still had no idea how she'd gotten there.

Then she looked to her left and held back a gasp in case anyone was listening. Both Aimee and Dawn were secured to the wall, their chains thick and covered in runes. Dhani figured the bonds had to be made for shifters. Somehow, whoever took Dhani, had taken her two friends also.

Dhani tried to scoot over to them, then realized that she was chained, as well, only her chains were much thinner than the others. But she was just far enough away from Aimee and Dawn that her very strong shifter friends couldn't break the links for her.

Whoever had kidnapped her and her friends knew what they were doing. Dhani was just thankful that Cheyenne hadn't made it to the cabin before everything happened.

Her head ached, and bile filled her throat as what had occurred in the cabin before she woke up here slammed into her.

She had thought she could trust Dave. When Kameron left, she'd been alone with the two soldiers that she thought she could trust. She'd been wrong. So very wrong.

Tino had been inside with her, going through some things in the cabin since the place hadn't really been used. She needed to keep busy, and it wasn't as if she could make up lesson plans at the moment. So she went to work de-cluttering, with Tino's help. She'd known he was placating her so she wouldn't be alone, but now she wished he'd have stayed in a safer place. Because after ten minutes of cleaning, Dave had walked inside—though he should have been on patrol—and Tino had turned, his eyes wide, asking why Dave was inside and not out on watch.

And then there was blood.

So much blood.

Tino had knocked her to the side to protect her. The action had her hitting her head against the wall, and she'd gotten slightly dizzy but was still trying to help. Dave and

Tino fought, knocking everything to the ground, breaking windows, smashing furniture. And then Dave had slashed into Tino's belly, gutting him. And then he slashed again. And again.

Until Tino wasn't able to fight back.

Then Dave had come for her.

Looking down, she was still covered in her friend's blood, but she didn't seem hurt. She was pretty sure Dave had knocked her out again, but he hadn't hurt her beyond that.

Apparently, the man Dave had been working for all this time wanted to do the hurting himself.

And they had taken her friends, as well.

She knew Kameron would come. Just like she knew that Walker and Mitchell would be on their way, too. They would be able to feel the bond between themselves and their mates and know that something was wrong. They would also know that only a Packmate could've taken her friends. Because they had been safe inside the den wards.

Because they had a traitor.

One they hadn't even considered could turn.

But he had.

And now Dhani knew why she'd felt as if she shouldn't be in the den. Why she might have been able to keep some people safe, but not everyone. Tino was dead because of her. All because Dave was working for someone else.

There was nothing she could do to change those facts.

The door opened, and a woman with long, red hair strolled in as if she hadn't a care in the world. As if there weren't three women—one covered in blood—chained in a basement with moldy water and rats running around. Of course, the rats were only near Dhani and not the two shifters in the room, but she was doing her best not to think about that.

"You're awake. Good. I knocked the others out a little harder than you. Just takes a little magic. I'm good at that. Either way, they're not going to be a problem for a long while. And if Blade lets me, they won't be a problem at all soon. You, on the other hand, are exactly who we wanted. And we can't just let you die like we're going to do with these girls. You're going to be special. Very, very special."

"I wish you would stop telling them all our plans. Or at least part of them." A huge man with a buzz cut and a scar on his face pushed his way into the small basement and glared at the woman. Dhani knew exactly where she was now. This had to be Blade, a very dominant wolf and the Aspen Pack Alpha. The woman with the red hair beside him was his fire witch, Scarlett. The Talons had hoped she was dead because her shifter mate had died in a previous bout. Not the case, apparently. Somehow, she'd found her way back, probably doing something dark that Dhani didn't want to think about. And Dhani was the only one of her friends awake to witness what they were about to do next. She hoped to hell that her mate and the others got there soon. Because Dhani was human, and she was afraid that she wouldn't be strong enough to fight them. At least, not for long.

"Well, while you figure out exactly what needs to be

done with the two shifters, I'm going to check on the little human who has to die the right way. Because while you say she's human, there's something different about her. I can't quite put my finger on it, though. You're not a little witch, are you, little girl?"

Her, a witch? There was no way. Kameron had thought there might be some witch blood in her ancestry. But even as everything that had happened started to come at her again—the dreams, the *knowing*, the way she reacted to the wards, the way her bond with Kameron felt—she still didn't think she could be a witch. Because wouldn't she have powers? Some kind of magic? She had spent time around some of the other witches within the den, and they'd never said anything about her. Of course, when she was with them, she'd been surrounded by tons of magic. Maybe the wards and other things had masked her power? But she still didn't believe whatever this woman, this Scarlett, said.

"I'm no witch. But if you hurt me, the Talons will kill you."

The fire witch rolled her eyes, and Blade just growled. Maybe that wasn't the right thing to say, but what was she supposed to do? She didn't have a weapon, and both of her friends who were far stronger than her were knocked out with some sort of magical spell. All she had were her words and her wits. Hopefully, soon, she would have her mate. She just hoped he didn't get hurt because of her because she would never forgive herself if that happened.

She was finding it hard to forgive herself for Tino as it was.

219

"If she's a witch, then she's of no use to us. Figure out exactly what she is. If she's human, then she's mine. If she's a witch? Then she's all yours."

Chills raced down her body at the Alpha's words. How the hell had her life turned into this?

Blade shrugged as if Dhani's life meant nothing, and to him, it didn't. He was an insane wolf who wanted power and would stop at nothing to get it. No wonder Kameron wanted this man dead.

Before she could think about what she was going to say next, the fire witch held up her hands, palms out, and chanted something Dhani didn't understand. Power slammed into her, burning her flesh, searing the magic into her skin.

She screamed, and then…darkness.

And then she was there. Right where she started. In a dream that wasn't a dream.

"Granddaughter."

Dhani should have known all along. She could see her eyes in this woman, the shape, the color, the intensity the same as hers. She could see how the older woman smiled in a way that reminded Dhani of her own mother.

The old woman, the woman from her dreams, was her grandmother.

She should have known.

But she hadn't.

She had no idea what she was doing here now. She had no idea where *here* was.

"You? It's been you all this time? Why couldn't you just

tell me what you want me to know? Where are we? Why does it still hurt?"

"I'm so sorry. I'm *so* sorry, my Dhanielle. It hurts because you're still alive. It hurts because you're still fighting. Because of the blood that runs in your veins. The blood I tried to protect. And that is what he wants, what you must protect, my child. I've met you before, Dhanielle. As a baby. I helped welcome you into this world after your mother, my daughter, gave birth to you. I saw the strength in your eyes, such spirit, such will. I also saw your death. I saw that, one day, you would die for your mate. You would burn in agony, and the world would crumble. Because your death would start it all. You wouldn't have found the women who became your closest friends. Because you would've hidden yourself in the world of magic just like my daughter was forced to do. Just like I was forced to do. You still would've found Kameron, fate always has a way. But he wouldn't have been the same man. You wouldn't have been the same woman. And when you died for him, and war came—too early, too fast, and too late—the world would've ended. And not just my world. I had to stop that. I'm sorry I couldn't tell you. But I wasn't here. I wasn't there."

Dhani didn't understand, but somehow, parts of it made sense. She knew she didn't know everything, though, and she couldn't find the words to speak. It didn't matter, however, her grandmother wasn't done.

"That scar on your side, it's from the binding. It won't go away, I'm afraid."

Dhani sucked in a breath. That wisp of flame, the mark

that she'd always wondered about. The one that Kam had touched that sent her over the edge.

"I never wanted this world for you. I wanted you to find happiness. But I think I stripped something vital from your life. From my own child's life. I knew it had to be done. I knew the magic that pulsated in me wouldn't be enough. You are such a strong woman, my Dhanielle. So strong, so fierce. Your mate will come for you. He will fight. But you will not die for him. Not yet. But you must know that sacrifice does truly beget sacrifice. I had to bind your powers. Had to bind the powers of your mother and father. And in so doing, I had to strip the memories of who they once were so they wouldn't find out about the magic that pulsated in their veins. I had to hide who you were from so many. The red witch only knows that you possess magic because the binding is starting to fail like I always knew it would one day. Perhaps this is the right time for it to do so. Because you are not the same woman who would've died in agony. You are so much stronger. I just hope you understand."

She didn't. But it wasn't as if she knew where to start. Her parents had been witches? Just like she apparently was? No wonder they'd always felt like something was missing. Because they hadn't been the people they once were. If Dhani's death were truly a linchpin in some version of the future where war reigned, maybe it made sense.

Because this wasn't just a dream where her inner mind was making things up. Out of everything, this she knew.

She understood why her grandmother did what she did, but it still hurt to think about. She knew it would take longer than whatever moments they had together now for her to put everything together enough to get over it and move on. Because she was nowhere close.

She just needed Kameron.

The fact that that thought even came to her, told her she definitely wasn't the same person she was even a month ago.

"What does that all mean? I'm a witch?"

"You will be. You *are*. You're a spirit witch. The rarest of them all. We hide from others because not everyone likes our connection to the other worlds and to things they don't understand. We have *power*, my darling. But never forget, with power comes weakness."

Dhani still felt so far behind but knew she couldn't stop asking questions. How had she gotten to this point in her life? When she thought that things were going too fast for her by moving to the den and mating with Kameron, she'd been wrong. *This* was moving too fast.

"What can I do?"

This woman had called her strong. She sure as hell didn't feel like it just then.

"You'll know what to do when the time is right. Remember my words. My prophecy that is now yours. You stood up. You stood up to Kameron. You stood up to the world around you. You made a choice, to come to the den, to tell Kameron that you were strong. To tell the humans who were against you that you were strong. You stood up and put yourself amongst people, within a den that could truly be yours. You were missing so much in your life because of what I was forced to do, but you stood up."

Stand up.

The first part of the prophecy.

"Then you opened yourself up. You knew that things could be different, that you might be moving too fast, that you could be going in the wrong direction, but you still opened up for your mate. Without that bond, without that connection, you wouldn't be who you are today. You wouldn't be who you *need* to be today."

Open up.

The second part.

The only things left were for her to give up...and for a sacrifice. Dhani wasn't sure she wanted to know what those meant.

"As for give up, that is something you'll know soon. Something I know you are finally strong enough to handle. I'm sorry I can't help. I'm sorry that you only saw visions of my own visions. Because binding the powers of three powerful witches and taking away those memories took too much out of me. I bound and locked away your magic. I locked down all the magic I could, but then I was no more. Because sacrifice begets sacrifice, and it's not over yet. Be strong, Dhanielle. Be who I couldn't be. Be who your mother and your father once were before I was forced to change it all. Because they would've died long ago if I hadn't changed everything. And I will never forgive myself for doing what I had to do. But know that I love you. Know that I love them. And know that it's not over. You are strong, my

Dhanielle. So strong. Be strong and wake up. And save the world."

And then, Dhani woke up, her eyes wide as the witch in front of her opened her mouth and screamed.

"No, it can't be true."

Dhani knew she was a witch, yet her powers were still bound to whatever her grandmother had done. She just knew. But now the witch knew, too.

Before she could figure out what to do next, Aimee and Dawn were suddenly awake, fighting against their chains next to her as the door slammed open. Kameron, Max, and Cheyenne stood in the doorway, light surrounding them, and then she knew it was over.

Maybe they had a chance.

Maybe.

CHAPTER TWENTY-ONE

K ameron howled, Max joining him by his side. Cheyenne let out a very inhuman growl, and he wanted to curse that she was there. But she hadn't allowed them to leave her behind, promising that she'd stay out of the way and only use her skills as a vet to help, but now that she was there, ready to fight, he knew that he might have made a mistake.

But his wolf only had eyes for Dhani. His mate. His *chained* mate.

Fuck. This.

He'd followed his mate bond to a cellar that almost looked like a basement. Blade, four or five wolves, and the red witch stood in one area. Dhani, Aimee, and Dawn were chained, fucking *chained* to the walls in the opposite corner.

Blood would be spilled today, and it wouldn't be his.

Fuck. This.

He repeated the words to himself before he jumped. But as soon as he did, a familiar wolf, a wolf that broke part of him deep inside, slammed into his chest. The action brought him down on his back outside of the cellar. Max grabbed Cheyenne and rolled to the other side before pushing her away to fight the other wolves that had come out of the brush and up from the cellar to attack them.

Fuck. The witch had hidden everyone's scents, but Kameron hadn't been able to wait for their own witches and backup to arrive before he tried to save his mate and the others. His family was on the way, but they were still at least twenty minutes out. Kameron and Max had been closer, and Gideon had told them to hold the line.

He just prayed to the goddess that they could actually accomplish that.

Dave snapped his fangs at him, and Kameron punched the man he had trusted in the face. The other man had shifted part of his face as well as his claws, telling Kam that the wolf was pretty dominant. But not as dominant as Kam. He had to blink away the images of Tino's dead body from his mind. He'd been forced to leave the other man at the cabin, alone and growing cold. He knew there were other Pack members out there now, making sure to pay the other man the respect he deserved. Because the way the room had been destroyed, Tino had given his life to save Dhani's.

And that meant Dave had to die.

No matter what.

Dave punched at him, but Kam was stronger. Faster. He

gripped the other man's fist and squeezed. The bones broke under his strength, and Dave screamed.

Then Kameron rolled and flipped the other man onto his back, pressing down on his neck with a forearm. "Why? Why did you betray us?"

"Fuck. You."

"Wrong answer."

Then he snapped the man's neck, making the death quick because, as much as Kameron might want the other man to suffer, he wasn't evil. And Max needed help with the Aspens who had come out of the woodwork. Maybe if they weren't surrounded and weren't on the losing end of whatever the hell was going on, Kam would have been able to get answers. But they weren't, and he wasn't going to let his anger and vengeance get in the way.

Max fought off two wolves, using his newly learned and adapted fighting skills to protect Cheyenne's and Kameron's backs. Cheyenne had a knife and was stabbing any of the foes that Max laid at her feet. It was an oddly decent way of fighting, and Kameron was not only surprised but also happy to see it. Cheyenne could hold her own. All of them could.

So Kameron fought by their sides, all the while trying to get closer to the cellar door so he could get to Dhani and the others. He couldn't see her, but he could feel her, scent her.

A gunshot split the air, and Kameron snapped the neck of the wolf in front of him before turning to Blade.

Blade had the three women on chains behind him. They weren't on their knees, but rather on their feet, fighting and growling. Kam and Max both went to lunge when Cheyenne called out.

"No. Look. The witch."

Kameron cursed when he looked at Scarlett, the witch who was supposed to be dead. She had her hands covered in flame and was pointing at the three women, essentially forcing Max and Kameron to stand down.

"The humans were supposed to take you out, but it seems I'm going to have to do it." Blade spat on the ground. "You were never strong enough. That's why you and the Redwoods haven't fought me. Now, you'll see my strength."

"You have women on *chains* behind you, and you call yourself strong?" Kameron asked. "A real man, a real *wolf* wouldn't resort to that. They'd fight me head-on rather than using leverage to keep me at bay."

Blade's eyes glowed gold. "You've always been in my way. Just like your fucking Alpha and the rest of you Brentwoods. None of you deserve the limelight. None of you deserve the reverence the other wolves and the humans give you. Soon, the world will see the truth. Soon, they'll see it all. You couldn't even see that it wasn't the humans that tried to kill you and your human bitch mate. It was Dave after Scarlett used her magic on him. It was always him. He was tired of the Brentwoods always telling him what to do and never giving him the position he wanted. You made him a sentry. I gave him *power.*"

Well, that answered that.

"Fight me like the Alpha you say you are. Fight me and let the others go. I'm what you want."

"I want Gideon's head on my desk."

"You'll have to settle for me."

Blade grinned. "Deal." He turned to his other wolves. There were only four others, and Kameron thought that was odd. Maybe the whole Pack wasn't on their Alpha's side. But that was something they'd have to deal with when they got out of this. "Don't kill the women. Just the half-wolf mongrel that no matter how many parts they chop off of him, can't seem to die. Leave the asshole Enforcer to me."

Then Blade leapt.

Kameron lunged out of the way, letting his claws out to fight with all his strength. Dhani yelled from her spot, and from the corner of his eye, he saw Cheyenne throw a rock at Scarlett's head. Somehow, the witch hadn't seen her, and Scarlett went to her knees.

Damn good throw.

Cheyenne immediately went to the women's sides and tried to get their chains off. Dhani's looked to be weaker than the others, and he had a feeling between the four of them, they'd be free soon.

Thank the goddess.

He saw all of that without truly looking, his attention on the far stronger wolf in front of him. There were many reasons why his Pack hadn't fought Blade and the Aspens head-on. Blade's strength was the main part of it.

Because Kameron wasn't strong enough to fight Blade alone. The only way he figured he might live through this was if, somehow, his Pack made it to them on time. Or if Max could fight off his wolves and the women got free, away from the witch, and were able to help. It wouldn't be easy, and he wasn't going down without a fight. He'd use every ounce of energy and strength he had, and he would damn well try to win.

Blade clawed at Kameron's chest, and though he moved quickly, it wasn't quick enough. Kam let out a growl as his blood scented the air. Blade grinned in triumph, but Kameron wasn't done. Kam lowered his shoulder and ran into Blade's gut. They both hit the ground, rolling. Blade punched and kicked and used his claws. Kameron fought back, trying to get the advantage, but he knew he wasn't strong enough.

And he resented the hell out of it.

They rolled again, Blade pressing down on Kameron's chest, and Kameron felt a few ribs snap. He sucked in a ragged breath, knowing that one of the bones had pierced his lung. He'd be okay. For now. He'd need Walker to Heal him soon or he might not heal at all, but he still had time. He just had to make it.

Then Blade had his hands around Kameron's throat, and Kameron used his claws to dig deep gouges into the man's arms. Kameron gasped for breath, his body shaking as he tried to pull the Alpha away, but that was the difference between an Alpha and an Enforcer.

Kameron just wasn't strong enough.

But he was also a Pack wolf, and that meant he wasn't alone.

Max ripped Blade off of Kameron, and Kameron rolled to his feet, ignoring the pain and the fact that he couldn't catch a full breath. He needed to stop Blade. Needed to protect his mate.

Needed to do it all.

Even if it took everything he had to accomplish it.

"You're all insane!" Scarlett yelled with a laugh. "And that's why you wolves will never win. It takes a *witch*!"

Blade stopped fighting. Max stopped fighting. The three remaining living wolves that Max hadn't killed stopped fighting. The women stopped fighting.

Because Scarlett spread her arms and screamed.

And flames shot toward them all. Toward Blade. Toward the Aspens. Toward Max. Toward Cheyenne. Toward Dawn. Toward Aimee. Toward Dhani. Toward his mate.

"Dhani!" he shouted.

But it was too late.

Dhani stood in front of them all, her hair blowing in a wind he couldn't see, couldn't feel. When she crossed her arms over her chest, he didn't understand, then she spread her arms, and his world shifted.

Silence reigned.

And the flames engulfed her in one breath.

And into the next.

And then, there was nothing.

CHAPTER TWENTY-TWO

S tand up.
  Open up.
  Give up.
Sacrifice begets sacrifice.

Dhani knew what she needed to do. The fire would come. The magic would come, and she would be the sacrifice. But unlike the visions of her grandmother before the binding, this would not be the end.

Because she was a witch. A spirit witch. One who spoke with the dead, who touched the magic of others and saw beneath it.

The flames licked her skin, just like in the dream, but it didn't hurt. Others screamed and shouted around her, but this wasn't the end. Dhani tilted her head to the side, studying the magic around her. She had no idea how she *knew*—then again, this was her, so she went with her gut.

She wrapped the flames around her arms and pulled and then pushed. Instead of the flames going around her and enveloping her friends and family, instead of the fire burning her mate, she sent it back to its creator.

Scarlett screamed, the fire surrounding the witch who had never truly understood, who had never really felt the flame. And then she was no more. She was just ash, and the fire slid away, turning to smoke and a past she knew she would always be entangled with.

She was a spirit witch. A formidable power. A mate. A woman who would and could protect all.

The war wasn't won. It wasn't over. The battle wasn't even finished, but this time, she could fight back.

Finally.

"Dhani!" Kameron was at her side as the smoke faded. He cupped her face. "What the fuck? I mean, goddess, Dhani."

"I'm a witch." She swallowed hard. "Long story."

He snorted, kissed her hard, then turned to where Blade was coming at him. "I want to hear it. After we finish this."

She gripped his arm. "Deal."

Even more wolves came out of the woods. Soon, there were a dozen Aspens against the rest of the Talons. Dhani had no idea what she was doing with her powers, but she could somehow create a shield that could protect her friends and mate for short bursts. For now, she was working on instinct, and one day, when everything finally hit her, she'd learn more. She knew she would because that was who she was, but for now, she would just do what she could and try to stay out of the way, as well.

She knew her mate was hurting to the point where his breathing was labored, and she could feel the pain along the bond. Max was bloody, and he had Cheyenne by his side, stabbing anyone he threw to her. Dhani honestly didn't know how the two were doing it, but when Max couldn't get the killing blow because the other wolf came at his bad side, he'd find a way to make it so Cheyenne was there to help. Her friend was a woman of healing, and Dhani knew that all of them wouldn't be walking away from this battle whole, but she would do her best to make sure they all made it out *alive*.

Dawn and Aimee had been training to fight in their animal and human forms and were working as a team against two of the Aspens who had come at them. They were winning because they weren't fighting each other like the two Aspens were. The two males seemed to be dominants, yet not as good at fighting as Dhani thought they should be. Or maybe *she* was running out of energy because she was pushing everything she had into her new magic and keeping the mating bond as full as she could to give Kameron strength. She noticed that every time she pushed some energy along the bond, Kameron could breathe easier. She knew she wouldn't be able to do it forever, but as long as she could give him what she had, he could fight Blade.

"Kam! Behind you!" she screamed as a final wolf jumped at him, and Kameron turned to slam the wolf to the ground. Dhani found herself facing Blade, who grinned at her.

"Little witch, you shouldn't be here. Seems you have more than you bargained for. Come with me and you'll be with a real man. Not this trash who can't even fight me like a true Alpha."

"Fuck. You."

"Couldn't have said it better myself, baby," Kam growled. Then he flung himself at Blade, and she fell to her knees, her energy waning. She knew she didn't have much left in her, but she wasn't going to stop until her mate and her family were safe.

Kameron sliced Blade's face open, blood pouring to the ground below them, and then Blade threw Kam back. He slid along the bloody ground into her, and she wrapped her arms around his shoulders.

And just when she thought that Blade would land the killing blow, the other man staggered to his feet, covered his ruined face with his hand, and ran.

The asshole *ran* away. If he'd been in wolf form, he'd probably have had his tail tucked between his legs.

Dhani blinked as the others on Blade's side ran behind their Alpha, leaving her people surrounding her, shaking. Then she heard the chopper blades, and knew the real reason Blade and his people had retreated.

"We need to go. We can't be here when the humans come, or we won't be able to answer their questions." Max held out his hand for Kam, and her mate slowly, achingly made his way to his feet.

"It's not over. But it is for today." Her mate helped her to her feet and, somehow, the group of them made it through the trees and to Max's SUV before the helicopter landed and the humans found more than they bargained for. Dhani didn't know what would come of it, but she knew that soon they'd have to answer the tough questions.

As soon as they got to the SUV, three other vehicles drove up, but they belonged to the Pack. Walker and Mitchell jumped out, running to their mates, but Max somehow got everyone into the right vehicles and on their way to the den and out of danger.

Dhani knew Kameron would have normally been the one to order people around, but she knew he was fading just as fast as she was. She leaned into his hold, thankful that Walker was beside them, doing his duty and Healing.

Warmth spread over her, and she closed her eyes as she let her body relax into her mate.

They had fought. They had bled. But she hadn't stopped. She hadn't let her fear of the visions and what was to come take over. She knew that Kameron wasn't happy that Blade had gotten away, but they'd fought.

They'd won in her mind, because they hadn't backed down, and all her people were alive.

Bloody and broken, but alive.

And that had to count for something.

It had to.

CHEYENNE

Cheyenne wanted to go home, but once she did, she was afraid that she wouldn't leave. Instead, she stood in the clinic's bathroom, staring at herself in the mirror. Bruises covered her arms and side, but that was from when Max had thrown her to the ground. She didn't blame him for that. He'd saved her life.

And in the end, she'd saved his, as well.

He'd let her fight by his side, a man she knew didn't let anyone do anything for him if he could help it. But in doing so, she'd taken a life. She'd taken more than one life.

Who was this person in the mirror?

How had this happened to her?

She was a vet. A woman of medicine and healing. And yet she'd taken lives to save lives.

She wasn't sure she could come to terms with that. This

wasn't her world, wasn't her reality. And yet she'd become immersed in it.

Over the past few months, she'd tried to find her balance as she had one foot in her human world and the other in the world of the paranormal. But she was afraid that she'd never find the balance she actually needed. She didn't think she was strong enough, didn't think she would end up sane enough.

Now that Dhani was mated and, apparently, a witch, she wouldn't age. Dawn wouldn't age. Aimee wouldn't age.

They would all stay as they were, and they would find their true happiness in a world where they were connected on a level she would never comprehend.

And Cheyenne would be left behind.

Again.

Maybe it was time for her to be the one to walk away. Before she lost herself. Before she lost them. Before she lost it all.

Maybe it was time for her to take that step.

Maybe.

CHAPTER TWENTY-THREE

Kameron could breathe, he could stretch, and he could see. But he knew this wasn't the end of it, not when Blade was still out there, and the world was getting that much darker.

But he had his mate, had his Dhani, so that had to count for something.

And it sure as hell did.

Somehow, the humans hadn't come after the Talons for what had happened at the cellar. Nor, from what they could see, had they gone after the Aspens. Kam wasn't sure if the human world even knew how close the Aspens were to the brink. And maybe that was a good thing. Because once the world knew about Blade and his plans, everything would change—and not for the better.

Perhaps those who were watching them were starting to understand that some things weren't for human consumption, weren't for their eyes. He didn't know exactly what would come next, but he had a feeling it would be big, whatever it was.

However, he didn't have the burning need to go out and take care of it himself like he once had. He knew he needed to rely on his Pack, his family. Because he couldn't do everything on his own—something Gideon had been trying to explain to him for what felt like years. He had a mate now, someone who had fought by his side and was still learning herself and her own strengths.

The Talons would win, he was sure of it. Even if they had to endure some pain along the way.

His bruises might have faded, but he still hurt from the idea that he'd trusted the wrong man. Dave was dead, and could no longer betray them. But no matter how many times others said it wasn't Kameron's fault that he hadn't been able to see the treachery, he knew he'd still shoulder the blame for a long time to come.

But he wouldn't do it alone.

"You're scowling," Gideon said from the other side of the living room. The Brentwoods had gathered once again at Gideon and Brie's, and this time, Kameron didn't feel like the odd man out. Everyone had brought their mates—though the children were at daycare since the adults were discussing war and death and the pups needed to retain their innocence for as long as possible. Max was the only one without a mate, but with so many family members around making sure he was included, it didn't feel like something was lacking...yet.

"I'm always scowling," Kam said deadpan.

Dhani pinched his side, and he narrowed his eyes as he looked down at her.

"What?"

"You don't always scowl. But why are you doing it now?"

He shrugged, squeezing his mate at the same time. Just a gentle squeeze, but his wolf needed to know that she was okay after everything that had happened. It would take a long while before Kam and his wolf were ready to let her out of their sight. Thankfully, Dhani not only understood but didn't want him out of her sight either.

"Just thinking about what to do next."

Brie leaned into Gideon as she studied him. "With Scarlett dead, as well as a few of Blade's top men, things are about to come to a head, I think."

"But he ran, right?" Ryder asked. He and Leah were sharing the smaller couch with Kameron and Dhani. Leah had been over at the house every evening since they came home, doing her best to help Dhani with her new powers. He had a feeling that Leah was going to become one of Dhani's closest friends before long, and he figured that was a good thing. Because the idea that his mate was a witch hadn't been surprising in the end. Her raw power, however, was startling, and something they all needed to get used to —and she needed to get a handle on.

She would, though. He didn't think his mate would allow anything less.

"He did," Max put it. "Kameron clawed up his face, and Blade ran as soon as the choppers sounded."

"He's still fucking strong, you guys," Kameron added. "Don't think just because he ran that he's weak." He hated the idea that Blade was indeed stronger than he was. But that was the difference between an Enforcer and an Alpha. Only Gideon and maybe Kade, the Redwood Alpha, would be able to stop Blade unless a new player came into the game and changed everything.

"He's strong, but together, we're stronger," Finn said from the comm where he and Brynn were streaming in from the Redwood den. They might not technically be Talons, but the Redwoods and Talons were so interconnected it was hard to see where one Pack ended and the other began. Kameron knew they would all be meeting with the Redwood hierachy soon for a battle plan, and he was ready for it. Today's meeting was just an informal family gathering where their wolves, cats, and other powers could get settled in, knowing they were safe...at least for now.

"Damn straight," Shane said from his perch on the couch beside Bram and Charlotte. With everything going on in the den and outside it, Shane was never far from Gideon's side these days. He was the official lieutenant that covered their Alpha to the point where he and his mates were practically living with the Alpha couple. It was working for now, and once they had Blade taken care of, hopefully, things would go back to their normal—whatever that was.

Brandon and Parker sat in front of them on the floor, Avery in their laps. She'd had headaches recently with so many visions bouncing back and forth, one after another. That was another reason they were having this meeting because she couldn't tell them exactly what would happen next, only that a huge game-changer was coming.

What that was? They didn't know, but Kameron didn't have a good feeling about it.

"I'm going to have to pick up training shifts," Mitchell added after a moment. "I know we're stronger than we've ever been, but I want to work things around so we all get rest and still find ways to keep up our strength."

"I'll help you figure out the plans," Dawn said from his side. "We'll make it work."

His cousin kissed the top of her head before relaxing a little. It was odd to see Mitchell anywhere near relaxed, even in this atmosphere, and Kameron was glad that he had Dawn to help him do that.

"I'm also going to need to start training up field medics again," Walker said with a hint of disgust so unlike him, it took Kam a minute to remember that Dave had been one of those medics in the previous battles. It seemed as if it wasn't just Kameron who felt Dave's betrayal deep in his soul.

"You're afraid we're going to need them more than ever," Aimee said, and it wasn't a question.

"From what Avery's said, yeah." Walker tucked his mate close, and Kameron did the same with Dhani.

His family had been through Hell and back, yet they had grown tremendously over the last few years. They'd come from the deepest parts of despair and pain and had clawed their way out to become one of the toughest and strongest Packs out there.

Only they weren't the strongest in the area. That title

was held by the Aspens. And with what Avery was seeing and how everything had panned out over the last few years, Kameron and his Pack would soon see what came from two or three Packs with such strength fighting head to head.

There would be no more hiding. No more trying to wait it out until they uncovered all the information.

"We're going to have to take Blade out," Gideon said with a growl. "There's no other way." Brie squeezed his hand, and Kameron knew she was scared. Because of all the people in this room, only her mate, Kameron's Alpha, had a chance of besting Blade.

"For Pack," Kam said softly.

"For Pack," the others answered.

And it was true. They would do anything for their Pack. No matter what. No matter the cost. He just prayed to the moon goddess that the cost wasn't so great that they lost everything in the end.

They didn't know what was to come with Blade. The other wolf might have lost his witch, but he still had an army, a Pack that could take out numerous others without breaking a sweat. The Aspens hadn't been forced to deal with a demon and a dark Pack like the Redwoods had. The Aspens hadn't been on the front lines during the war with the humans like the Talons had. They'd been able to build up their numbers, and now Blade was changing the game.

Kam still couldn't get in touch with their insider, Audrey, and he feared the worst. She'd risked her life and her sanity for Walker and Aimee, and now they might have lost her before they even had a chance to see how their alliance could work.

But as he looked around at his family and his mate, he knew that they were stronger than he and Blade had given them credit for.

They could handle this threat.

Because they had to.

They were fighters. They were Healers. They were wolves.

They were Pack.

They were Talons.

And they would not give up.

Ever.

CHAPTER TWENTY-FOUR

Dhani arched her back as Kameron slid into her one final time. "Yes, fill me. Take me."

Kam kissed the spot he'd just bitten, then whispered into her ear, "Always."

And when she came around his cock, he came with her, filling her up until they were both sweaty, a little messy, and beyond sated.

"I think you broke me," Kam muttered against her neck, and she laughed.

"You broke me first." She pushed at his massive shoulders. "Get off me, you big wolf. I need to breathe."

He laughed then rolled with her so she was splayed over his chest, and she didn't mind one bit. They only had an hour or so before they had to go back to their normal lives. The pups needed a teacher, and Kam needed to head back to the war room. And then, after that, she needed to train.

Not only with her new powers but also in hand-to-hand because she'd be damned if she would let Kameron fight without her.

She had no idea how to use her powers. The whole force field thing was actually much harder than expected, and she'd only gone on instinct in their time of need. She couldn't do it again, and it would be dangerous to try since she'd used too much of her energy making it happen the first time.

Kam hadn't been happy when Leah told them that.

But now, she was a witch. She knew her past, knew her family. Things were different now, but she knew this was who she was meant to be the whole time. A teacher. A witch. Kameron's mate. She wasn't going to be a wolf, and oddly, she was okay with that. She wasn't fully human, but she still had a hold on her humanity, and for her, that was what she needed.

And she'd also found out something else along the way. Something she hadn't known she needed. Her parents had also regained their magic *and* memories when the binding wore off. They'd come to the den right away, their eyes wide, begging her for forgiveness. There hadn't been anything to forgive. Leah had been right in that her parents had not only gone through hell in losing a part of themselves, but they had been hexed on top of it. Once the fire witch died, so had the hex.

Now, her parents were planning to move closer to the den and were looking into joining the Coven. They were rusty in their magic *and* in their relationship with their daughter. They'd learn again and, hopefully, would help Dhani in the process.

But they weren't the only ones trying to help her. She had a meeting with the Coven later to see if she could train with her parents and other spirit witches—if they could find them. Spirit witches were rare but coveted, and in this new world, her family wouldn't have to hide like they had before. For now, everyone was being super helpful and loving and caring—which was a change, apparently, from how things used to be.

Dhani had her morning with Kameron and didn't want it to end, but that evening, it was all about her and her girls for a dinner where they could come together and remember where they had been and face this new journey of theirs together. Cheyenne had said that she was busy and wouldn't be there, and Dhani was worried about that. But she wouldn't let her friend slip away, even if it would be hard. If Cheyenne needed them, then Dhani was stubborn enough to make sure they were there for their friend, even if the other woman didn't *want* to need them.

But now it was just about her and Kameron, in bed, their bodies pressed together, and their breathing slowing from their exertions. She'd never thought to have him in her life, never thought she'd have this kind of life at all. Yes, they'd found their way to each other in the most unconventional way, but that didn't mean it wasn't *right*.

She ran from fate for far too long, thinking she had to be the one to make all of her own choices. But now, she knew that fate had been right—at least in this instance.

"I love you," she whispered.

Kameron ran his hand down her back. "I love you, too. You're it for me, you know. Even if having you in my life is apparently costing me my street cred of being an asshole."

She levered herself up over him so she could smile into his face "Yeah? Well, I think once training starts again full-tilt, you'll get that asshole reputation back quickly."

"You say the sweetest things," he said with a laugh and then pulled her in for a kiss that once again took her breath away.

She loved this man, this wolf, with every ounce of her being. Because of him, because of her, she'd found all the pieces she'd been missing for so long.

And because she loved him, she knew that he was her most important piece.

The two of them had endured their paths before each other, but together, they would stake their claims along the path they forged.

She was his as much as he was hers. Their future, their present, and their past were all wrapped up and tangled with their bond.

And as her powers danced along her skin, she knew that she couldn't be happier—even with her grumpy wolf.

ALPHA

Blade turned on the system that the Voice of the Wolves, Parker of the Redwoods and Talons, had set up for each of the Packs. It was a way for all of them to communicate without the prying eyes of the humans.

And it was exactly what he needed.

He might not like the idea of using something that little spawn had made, but in the end, it would be for *his* benefit and would show the world whom he was.

He was done waiting for others to fall around him.

It was his time to show the others his full strength and what he held in his hand.

The camera faced him, and he gave a nod when the green light said that they were airing live.

"I am Blade, Alpha of the Aspen Pack. For too long, we have allowed others to weaken us, to dilute our lines to the point where we've been forced to hide away in secret, begging for scraps. We've allowed the humans to make the rules, to forge alliances where they pretend to have the power. I know you have watched this with horror and disdain, but know this...the time has come for change."

He paused for effect.

"And I am that change."

He pressed a button, not on the important piece in his right hand that he kept out of camera range, but on the trigger in his left. He knew the explosion would hit the airwaves soon, and the humans would know whom they were dealing with.

Only a few hundred would die, but they would know who their master was. It didn't matter where he placed the bomb. It only mattered that it had been placed.

"I am Blade, Alpha and ruler. And it is time for our people to come together under one sovereign, under someone who can protect and rule with an iron fist. Therefore, I am Blade of the Aspens no longer, but rather Blade, Supreme Alpha of all Packs who see this feed. Cross me and know my wrath. Cross this Pack and know the end. The time has come for true leadership. The time has come for a true ruler."

He snapped his teeth at the camera.

"The time has come for vengeance."

And as the other Alphas around the world either bowed in deference or howled with rage, Blade knew that this was only the first step. Because he could declare himself easily, but soon, the world would know *exactly* how he would maintain his rule.

One bloody Alpha at a time.

Coming Next in the Talon Pack World:
The Talon Pack ends with FOREVER BROKEN.

A NOTE FROM CARRIE ANN

Thank you so much for reading Strength Enduring! I do hope if you liked this story, that you would please leave a review! Reviews help authors and readers.

The Talon Pack is an ongoing series and not over yet. The final book, Forever Broken, will end the series with Max and Cheyenne.

Is that the last of the world that hols the Redwood Pack and the Talon Pack?

I sure hope not.

Just wait and see…

If you want to make sure you know what's coming next from me, you can sign up for my newsletter at www.CarrieAnnRyan.com; follow me on twitter at @CarrieAnnRyan, or like my Facebook page. I also have a Facebook Fan Club where we have trivia, chats, and other goodies. You guys are the reason I get to do what I do and I thank you.

Make sure you're signed up for my MAILING LIST so you can know when the next releases are available as well as find giveaways and FREE READS.

Happy Reading!

The Talon Pack:
  Book 1: Tattered Loyalties
  Book 2: An Alpha's Choice
  Book 3: Mated in Mist
  Book 4: Wolf Betrayed
  Book 5: Fractured Silence
  Book 6: Destiny Disgraced
  Book 7: Eternal Mourning
  Book 8: Strength Enduring
  Book 9: Forever Broken

ABOUT CARRIE ANN RYAN

Carrie Ann Ryan is the New York Times and USA Today bestselling author of contemporary and paranormal romance. Her works include the Montgomery Ink, Redwood Pack, Talon Pack, and Gallagher Brothers series, which have sold over 2.0 million books worldwide. She started writing while in graduate school for her advanced degree in chemistry and hasn't stopped since. Carrie Ann has written over fifty novels and novellas with more in the works. When she's not writing about bearded tattooed men or alpha wolves that need to find their mates, she's reading as much as she can and exploring the world of baking and gourmet cooking.

www.CarrieAnnRyan.com

MORE FROM CARRIE ANN RYAN

Montgomery Ink:

Book 7.5: Executive Ink
Book 8: Inked Memories
Book 8.5: Inked Nights
Book 8.7: Second Chance Ink

Montgomery Ink: Colorado Springs
Book 1: Fallen Ink
Book 2: Restless Ink
Book 3: Jagged Ink

The Gallagher Brothers Series:
A Montgomery Ink Spin Off Series
Book 1: Love Restored
Book 2: Passion Restored
Book 3: Hope Restored

The Whiskey and Lies Series:
A Montgomery Ink Spin Off Series
Book 1: Whiskey Secrets
Book 2: Whiskey Reveals
Book 3: Whiskey Undone

The Fractured Connections Series:
A Montgomery Ink Spin Off Series
Book 1: Breaking Without You

The Talon Pack:
Book 1: Tattered Loyalties

Book 2: An Alpha's Choice
Book 3: Mated in Mist
Book 4: Wolf Betrayed
Book 5: Fractured Silence
Book 6: Destiny Disgraced
Book 7: Eternal Mourning
Book 8: Strength Enduring
Book 9: Forever Broken

Redwood Pack Series:
Book 1: An Alpha's Path
Book 2: A Taste for a Mate
Book 3: Trinity Bound
Redwood Pack Box Set (Contains Books 1-3)
Book 3.5: A Night Away
Book 4: Enforcer's Redemption
Book 4.5: Blurred Expectations
Book 4.7: Forgiveness
Book 5: Shattered Emotions
Book 6: Hidden Destiny
Book 6.5: A Beta's Haven
Book 7: Fighting Fate
Book 7.5: Loving the Omega
Book 7.7: The Hunted Heart
Book 8: Wicked Wolf
The Complete Redwood Pack Box Set (Contains Books 1-7.7)

The Branded Pack Series:
   (Written with Alexandra Ivy)
   Book 1: Stolen and Forgiven
   Book 2: Abandoned and Unseen
   Book 3: Buried and Shadowed

Dante's Circle Series:
   Book 1: Dust of My Wings
   Book 2: Her Warriors' Three Wishes
   Book 3: An Unlucky Moon
   The Dante's Circle Box Set (Contains Books 1-3)
   Book 3.5: His Choice
   Book 4: Tangled Innocence
   Book 5: Fierce Enchantment
   Book 6: An Immortal's Song
   Book 7: Prowled Darkness
   The Complete Dante's Circle Series (Contains Books 1-7)

Holiday, Montana Series:
   Book 1: Charmed Spirits
   Book 2: Santa's Executive
   Book 3: Finding Abigail
   The Holiday, Montana Box Set (Contains Books 1-3)
   Book 4: Her Lucky Love
   Book 5: Dreams of Ivory
   The Complete Holiday, Montana Box Set (Contains Books 1-5)

The Happy Ever After Series:

Flame and Ink

Ink Ever After

Single Title:

Finally Found You

EXCERPT: WHISKEY SECRETS

From New York Times Bestselling Author Carrie Ann Ryan's Whiskey and Lies

Whiskey Secrets

Shocking pain slammed into his skull and down his back. Dare Collins did his best not to scream in the middle of his own bar. He slowly stood up and rubbed the back of his head since he'd been distracted and hit it on the countertop. Since the thing was made of solid wood and thick as hell, he was surprised he hadn't given himself a concussion. But since he didn't see double, he had a feeling once his long night was over, he'd just have to make the throbbing go away with a glass of Macallan.

There was nothing better than a glass of smooth

whiskey or an ice-cold mug of beer after a particularly long day. Which one Dare chose each night depended on not only his mood but also those around him. So was the life of a former cop turned bartender.

He had a feeling he'd be going for the whiskey and not a woman tonight—like most nights if he were honest. It had been a long day of inventory and no-show staff members. Meaning he had a headache from hell, and it looked as if he'd be working open to close when he truly didn't want to. But that's what happened when one was the owner of a bar and restaurant rather than just a manager or bartender—like he was with the Old Whiskey Restaurant and Bar.

It didn't help that his family had been in and out of the place all day for one reason or another—his brothers and parents either wanting something to eat or having a question that needed to be answered right away where a phone call or text wouldn't suffice. His mom and dad had mentioned more than once that he needed to be ready for their morning meeting, and he had a bad feeling in his gut about what that would mean for him later. But he pushed that from his thoughts because he was used to things in his life changing on a dime. He'd left the force for a reason, after all.

Enough of that.

He loved his family, he really did, but sometimes, they— his parents in particular—gave him a headache.

Since his mom and dad still ran the Old Whiskey Inn above his bar, they were constantly around, working their tails off at odd jobs that were far too hard for them at their ages, but they were all just trying to earn a living. When they weren't handling business for the inn, they were fixing problems upstairs that Dare wished they'd let him help with.

While he'd have preferred to call it a night and head back to his place a few blocks away, he knew that wouldn't happen tonight. Since his bartender, Rick, had called in sick at the last minute—as well as two of Dare's waitresses from the bar—Dare was pretty much screwed.

And if he wallowed just a little bit more, he might hear a tiny violin playing in his ear. He needed to get a grip and get over it. Working late and dealing with other people's mistakes was part of his job description, and he was usually fine with that.

Apparently, he was just a little off tonight. And since he knew himself well, he had a feeling it was because he was nearing the end of his time without his kid. Whenever he spent too many days away from Nathan, he acted like a crabby asshole. Thankfully, his weekend was coming up.

"Solving a hard math problem over there, or just daydreaming? Because that expression on your face looks like you're working your brain too hard. I'm surprised I don't see smoke coming out of your ears." Fox asked as he walked up to the bar, bringing Dare out of his thoughts. Dare had been pulling drafts and cleaning glasses mindlessly while in his head, but he was glad for the distraction, even if it annoyed him that he needed one.

Dare shook his head and flipped off his brother. "Suck me."

The bar was busy that night, so Fox sat down on one of the empty stools and grinned. "Nice way to greet your customers." He glanced over his shoulder before looking back at Dare and frowning. "Where are Rick and the rest of your staff?"

Dare barely held back a growl. "Out sick. Either there's really a twenty-four-hour stomach bug going around and I'm going to be screwed for the next couple of days, or they're all out on benders."

Fox cursed under his breath before hopping off his stool and going around the side of the large oak and maple bar to help out. That was Dare's family in a nutshell—they dropped everything whenever one of them needed help, and nobody even had to ask for it. Since Dare sucked at asking for help on a good day, he was glad that Fox knew what he needed without him having to say it.

Without asking, Fox pulled up a few drink orders and began mixing them with the skill of a long-time barkeep. Since Fox owned the small town newspaper—the Whiskey Chronicle—Dare was still surprised sometimes at how deft his younger brother was at working alongside him. Of course, even his parents, his older brother Loch, and his younger sister Tabby knew their way around the bar.

Just not as well as Dare did. Considering that this was *his* job, he was grateful for that.

He loved his family, his bar, and hell, he even loved his little town on the outskirts of Philly. Whiskey, Pennsylvania was like most other small towns in his state where some parts were new additions, and others were old stone buildings from the Revolutionary or Civil war eras with add-ons —like his.

And with a place called Whiskey, everyone attached the label where they could. Hence the town paper, his bar, and most of the other businesses around town. Only Loch's business really stood out with Loch's Security and Gym down the street, but that was just like Loch to be a little different yet still part of the town.

Whiskey had been named as such because of its old bootlegging days. It used to be called something else, but since Prohibition, the town had changed its name and cashed in on it. Whiskey was one of the last places in the country to keep Prohibition on the books, even with the nationwide decree. They'd fought to keep booze illegal, not for puritan reasons, but because their bootlegging market had helped the township thrive. Dare knew there was a lot more to it than that, but those were the stories the leaders told the tourists, and it helped with the flare.

Whiskey was located right on the Delaware River, so it overlooked New Jersey but was still on the Pennsylvania side of things. The main bridge that connected the two states through Whiskey and Ridge on the New Jersey side was one of the tourist spots for people to drive over and walk so they could be in two states at once while over the Delaware River.

Their town was steeped in history, and close enough to where George Washington had crossed the Delaware that they were able to gain revenue on the reenactments for the tourists, thus helping keep their town afloat.

The one main road through Whiskey that not only housed Loch's and Dare's businesses but also many of the other shops and restaurants in the area, was always jammed with cars and people looking for places to parallel park. Dare's personal parking lot for the bar and inn was a hot commodity.

And while he might like time to himself some days, he knew he wouldn't trade Whiskey's feel for any other place. They were a weird little town that was a mesh of history and newcomers, and he wouldn't trade it for the world. His sister Tabby might have moved out west and found her love and her place with the Montgomerys in Denver, but Dare knew he'd only ever find his home here.

Sure, he'd had a few flings in Denver when he visited his sister, but he knew they'd never be more than one night or two. Hell, he was the king of flings these days, and that was for good reason. He didn't need commitment or attachments beyond his family and his son, Nathan.

Time with Nathan's mom had proven that to him, after all.

"You're still daydreaming over there," Fox called out from the other side of the bar. "You okay?"

Dare nodded, frowning. "Yeah, I think I need more caffeine or something since my mind keeps wandering." He pasted on his trademark grin and went to help one of the new arrivals who'd taken a seat at the bar. Dare wasn't the broody one of the family—that honor went to Loch—and he hated when he acted like it.

"What can I get you?" he asked a young couple that had

taken two empty seats at the bar. They had matching wedding bands on their fingers but looked to be in their early twenties.

He couldn't imagine being married that young. Hell, he'd never been married, and he was in his mid-thirties now. He hadn't married Monica even though she'd given him Nathan, and even now, he wasn't sure they'd have ever taken that step even if they had stayed together. She had Auggie now, and he had…well, he had his bar.

That wasn't depressing at all.

"Two Yuenglings please, draft if you have it," the guy said, smiling.

Dare nodded. "Gonna need to see your IDs, but I do have it on tap for you." As Yuengling was a Pennsylvania beer, not having it outside the bottle would be stupid even in a town that prided itself on whiskey.

The couple pulled out their IDs, and Dare checked them quickly. Since both were now the ripe age of twenty-two, he went to pull them their beers and set out their check since they weren't looking to run a tab.

Another woman with long, caramel brown hair with hints of red came to sit at the edge of the bar. Her hair lay in loose waves down her back and she had on a sexy-as-fuck green dress that draped over her body to showcase sexy curves and legs that seemed to go on forever. The garment didn't have sleeves so he could see the toned muscles in her arms work as she picked up a menu to look at it. When she looked up, she gave him a dismissive glance before focusing on the menu again. He held back a sigh.

Not in the mood to deal with whatever that was about, he let Fox take care of her and put her from his mind. No use dealing with a woman who clearly didn't want him near, even if it were just to take a drink order. Funny, he usually had to speak to a female before making her want him out of the picture. At least, that's what he'd learned from Monica.

And why the hell was he thinking about his ex again? He usually only thought of her in passing when he was talking to Nathan or hanging out with his kid for the one weekend a month the custody agreement let Dare have him. Having been in a dangerous job and then becoming a bartender didn't look good to some lawyers it seemed, at least when Monica had fought for full custody after Nathan was born.

He pushed those thoughts from his mind, however, not in the mood to scare anyone with a scowl on his face by remembering how his ex had looked down on him for his occupation even though she'd been happy to slum it with him when it came to getting her rocks off.

Dare went through the motions of mixing a few more drinks before leaving Fox to tend to the bar so he could go check on the restaurant part of the building.

Since the place had originally been an old stone inn on both floors instead of just the top one, it was set up a little differently than most newer buildings around town. The bar was off to one side; the restaurant area where they served delicious, higher-end entrees and tapas was on the other. Most people needed a reservation to sit down and eat in the main restaurant area, but the bar also had seating for dinner, only their menu wasn't quite as extensive and ran closer to bar food.

In the past, he'd never imagined he would be running something like this, even though his parents had run a smaller version of it when he was a kid. But none of his siblings had been interested in taking over once his parents wanted to retire from the bar part and only run the inn. When Dare decided to leave the force only a few years in, he'd found his place here, however reluctantly.

Being a cop hadn't been for him, just like being in a relationship. He'd thought he would be able to do the former, but life had taken a turn, and he'd faced his mortality far sooner than he bargained for. Apparently, being a gruff, perpetually single bar owner was more his speed, and he was pretty damn good at it, too. Most days, anyway.

His house manager over on the restaurant side was running from one thing to another, but from the outside, no one would have noticed. Claire was just that good. She was in her early fifties and already a grandmother, but she didn't look a day over thirty-five with her smooth, dark skin and bright smile. Good genes and makeup did wonders—according to her anyway. He'd be damned if he'd say that. His mother and Tabby had taught him *something* over the years.

The restaurant was short-staffed but managing, and he was grateful he had Claire working long hours like he did. He oversaw it all, but he knew he couldn't have done it without her. After making sure she didn't need anything, he headed back to the bar to relieve Fox. The rush was finally dying down now, and his brother could just sit back and enjoy a beer since Dare knew he'd already worked a long day at the paper.

By the time the restaurant closed and the bar only held a few dwindling costumers, Dare was ready to go to bed and forget the whole lagging day. Of course, he still had to close out the two businesses and talk to both Fox and Loch since his older brother had shown up a few moments ago. Maybe he'd get them to help him close out so he wouldn't be here until midnight. He must be tired if the thought of closing out was too much for him.

"So, Rick didn't show, huh?" Loch asked as he stood up from his stool. His older brother started cleaning up beside Fox, and Dare held back a smile. He'd have to repay them in something other than beer, but he knew they were working alongside him because they were family and had the time; they weren't doing it for rewards.

"Nope. Shelly and Kayla didn't show up either." Dare resisted the urge to grind his teeth at that. "Thanks for helping. I'm exhausted and wasn't in the mood to deal with this all alone."

"That's what we're here for," Loch said with a shrug.

"By the way, you have any idea what this seven a.m. meeting tomorrow is about?" Fox asked after a moment. "They're putting Tabby on speaker phone for it and everything."

Dare let out a sigh. "I'm not in the mood to deal with any meeting that early. I have no idea what it's going to be about, but I have a bad feeling."

"Seems like they have an announcement." Loch sat back down on his stool and scrolled through his phone. He was constantly working or checking on his daughter, so his phone was strapped to him at all times. Misty had to be with Loch's best friend, Ainsley, since his brother worked that night. Ainsley helped out when Loch needed a night to work or see Dare. Loch had full custody of Misty, and being a single father wasn't easy.

Dare had a feeling no matter what his parents had to say, things were going to be rocky after the morning meeting. His parents were caring, helpful, and always wanted the best for their family. That also meant they tended to be slightly overbearing in the most loving way possible.

"Well, shit."

It looked like he'd go without whiskey *or* a woman tonight.

Of course, an image of the woman with gorgeous hair and that look of disdain filled his mind, and he held back a sigh. Once again, Dare was a glutton for punishment, even in his thoughts.

The next morning, he cupped his mug of coffee in his hands and prayed his eyes would stay open. He'd stupidly gotten caught up on paperwork the night before and was now running on about three hours of sleep.

Loch sat in one of the booths with Misty, watching as she colored in her coloring book. She was the same age as Nathan, which Dare always appreciated since the cousins could grow up like siblings—on weekends when Dare had

Nathan that was. The two kids got along great, and he hoped that continued throughout the cootie phases kids seemed to get sporadically.

Fox sat next to Dare at one of the tables with his laptop open. Since his brother owned the town paper, he was always up-to-date on current events and was even now typing up something.

They had Dare's phone between them with Tabby on the other line, though she wasn't saying anything. Her fiancé, Alex, was probably near as well since those two seemed to be attached at the hip. Considering his future brother-in-law adored Tabby, Dare didn't mind that as much as he probably should have as a big brother.

The elder Collinses stood at the bar, smiles on their faces, yet Dare saw nervousness in their stances. He'd been a cop too long to miss it. They were up to something, and he had a feeling he wasn't going to like it.

"Just get it over with," Dare said, keeping his language decent—not only for Misty but also because his mother would still take him by the ear if he cursed in front of her.

But because his tone had bordered on rude, his mother still raised a brow, and he sighed. Yep, he had a really bad feeling about this.

"Good morning to you, too, Dare," Bob Collins said with a snort and shook his head. "Well, since you're all here, even our baby girl, Tabby—"

"Not a baby, Dad!" Tabby called out from the phone, and the rest of them laughed, breaking the tension slightly.

"Yeah, we're not babies," Misty put in, causing everyone to laugh even harder.

"Anyway," Barbara Collins said with a twinkle in her eye. "We have an announcement to make." She rolled her shoulders back, and Dare narrowed his eyes. "As you know, your father and I have been nearing the age of retirement for a while now, but we still wanted to run our inn as innkeepers rather that merely owners."

"Finally taking a vacation?" Dare asked. His parents worked far too hard and wouldn't let their kids help them. He'd done what he could by buying the bar from them when he retired from the force and then built the restaurant himself.

"If you'd let me finish, young man, I'd let you know," his mother said coolly, though there was still warmth in her eyes. That was his mother in a nutshell. She'd reprimand, but soothe the sting, too.

"Sorry," he mumbled, and Fox coughed to cover up a laugh. If Dare looked behind him, he figured he'd see Loch hiding a smile of his own.

Tabby laughed outright.

Damn little sisters.

"So, as I was saying, we've worked hard. But, lately, it seems like we've worked *too* hard." She looked over at his dad and smiled softly, taking her husband's hand. "It's time to make some changes around here."

Dare sat up straighter.

"We're retiring. Somewhat. The inn hasn't been doing as well as it did back when it was with your grandparents, and part of that is on the economy. But part of that is on us. What we want to do is renovate more and update the existing rooms and service. In order to do that and step back as innkeepers, we've hired a new person."

"You're kidding me, right?" Dare asked, frowning. "You can't just hire someone to take over and work in our building without even talking to us. And it's not like I have time to help her run it when she doesn't know how you like things."

"You won't be running it," Bob said calmly. "Not yet, anyway. Your mom and I haven't fully retired, and you know it. We've been running the inn for years, but now we want to step away. Something *you've* told us we should do. So, we hired someone. One who knows how to handle this kind of transition and will work with the construction crew and us. She has a lot of experience from working in Philly and New York and will be an asset."

Dare fisted his hands by his sides and blew out a breath. They had to be fucking kidding. "It sounds like you've done your research and already made your decision. Without asking us. Without asking *me*."

His mother gave him a sad look. "We've always wanted to do this, Dare, you know that."

"Yes. But you should have talked to us. And renovating like this? I didn't know you wanted to. We could have helped." He didn't know why he was so angry, but being kept out of the loop was probably most of it.

His father signed. "We've been looking into this for years, even before you came back to Whiskey and bought the bar from us. And while it may seem like this is out of the blue, we've been doing the research for a while. Yes, we should have told you, but everything came up all at once recently, and we wanted to show you the plans when we had details rather than get your hopes up and end up not doing it."

Dare just blinked. There was so much in that statement —in *all* of those statements—that he couldn't quite process it. And though he could have yelled about any of it just then, his mind fixed on the one thing that annoyed him the most.

"So, you're going to have some city girl come into *my* place and order me around? I don't think so."

"And why not? Have a problem with listening to women?"

Dare stiffened because that last part hadn't come from his family. No. He turned toward the voice. It had come from the woman he'd seen the night before in the green dress.

And because fate liked to fuck with him, he had a feeling he knew *exactly* who this person was.

Their newly hired innkeeper.

And new thorn in his side.

Find out more in Whiskey Secrets.
To make sure you're up to date on all of Carrie Ann's releases, sign up for her mailing list HERE.